RUNNING SCARED

A MYSTERY IN CARLSBAD CAVERNS NATIONAL PARK

GLORIA SKURZYNSKI AND ALANE FERGUSON

NATIONAL
GEOGRAPHIC
WASHINGTON, D.C.

To Tom "Boomer" Bemis,

a true hero and an inspiring role model

First digest edition paperback printing 2008
ISBN: 978-1-4263-0182-7
Text copyright © 2002 Gloria Skurzynski and Alane Ferguson
Cover illustration copyright © 2008 Jeffrey Mangiat

Map by Carl Mehler, Director of Maps
Map research and production by Joseph F. Ochlak and Equator Graphics

Mexican free-tailed bat art by Joan Wolbier

This is a work of fiction. Any resemblance to living persons or events other than
descriptions of natural phenomena is purely coincidental.

Library of Congress Cataloging-in-Publication Data

Skurzynski, Gloria.
Running scared / Gloria Skurzynski and Alane Ferguson.
p. cm. — (Mysteries in our national parks ; #11)
Summary: While lost in a tunnel at Carlsbad Cavern, thirteen-year-old Jack,
eleven-year-old Ashley, and their eight-year-old foster brother, Sam, think bats
and darkness are their worst problems, until they stumble across thieves.
ISBN 0-7922-6948-9 (pbk.)
ISBN 0-7922-8232-9
[1. Lost children—Fiction. 2. Bats—Fiction.
3. Carlsbad Caverns National Park (N.M.)—Fiction. 4. Foster home care—Fiction.
5. National parks and reserves—Fiction. 6. Mystery and detective stories.]
I. Ferguson, Alane. II. Title. III. Series.
PZ7.S6287 Ru 2002
[Fic]—dc21
2002005277

Printed in the United States of America

13/WOR-CML/2

ACKNOWLEDGMENTS

The authors are grateful to those at

Carlsbad Caverns National Park who shared

information and their expertise with us, especially Bob

Hoff, Park Historian;

Myra Barnes, Wildlife Biologist;

Stan Allison, Cave Resource Specialist;

David Roemer, Biologist;

Laura Denny, Park Ranger, Law Enforcement Division;

Stacey Haney, Park Ranger,

Interpretive Division;

and of course Tom Bemis

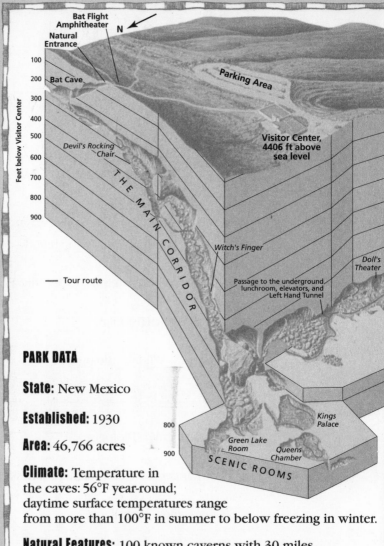

Bat Flight
Amphitheater

Natural
Entrance

N

Parking Area

Feet below Visitor Center

100
200 — Bat Cave
300
400
500
600 — Devil's Rocking Chair
700
800
900

Visitor Center,
4406 ft above
sea level

THE MAIN CORRIDOR

Witch's Finger

Doll's
Theater

— Tour route

Passage to the underground
lunchroom, elevators, and
Left Hand Tunnel

PARK DATA

State: New Mexico

Established: 1930

Area: 46,766 acres

800

Kings
Palace

Green Lake
Room

Queens
Chamber

900

SCENIC ROOMS

Climate: Temperature in
the caves: 56°F year-round;
daytime surface temperatures range
from more than 100°F in summer to below freezing in winter.

Natural Features: 100 known caverns with 30 miles
of passageways; stalagmites as high as 6-story buildings;
a chamber large enough to hold 14 football fields; a
population of roughly a half million Mexican free-tailed
bats that emerge nightly (May–October) to feed on insects.

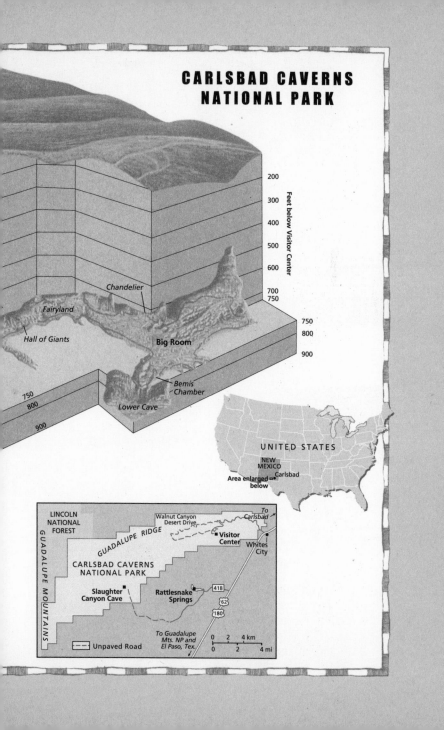

CARLSBAD CAVERNS NATIONAL PARK

Feet below Visitor Center

200
300
400
500
600
700
750

750
800
900

Chandelier

Fairyland

Hall of Giants

Big Room

Bemis Chamber

750
800
900

Lower Cave

UNITED STATES

NEW MEXICO

Carlsbad

Area enlarged below

LINCOLN NATIONAL FOREST

GUADALUPE RIDGE

Walnut Canyon Desert Drive

To Carlsbad

Visitor Center

Whites City

CARLSBAD CAVERNS NATIONAL PARK

GUADALUPE MOUNTAINS

Slaughter Canyon Cave

Rattlesnake Springs

418

62

180

To Guadalupe Mts. NP and El Paso, Tex.

--- Unpaved Road

0   2   4 km

0   2   4 mi

The light from his head-lantern cast deep shadows along the cave walls. Ink-black phantoms seemed to dance across formations like evil spirits, but the man wasn't afraid. Nothing scared him, except, perhaps, the thought of running out of money. Well, he didn't have to worry about that, not now. His flashlight felt heavy in his hand as he aimed it at the delicate cave balloon, as fragile and translucent as a soap bubble. It always amazed him what people would pay for a tiny thing like this. He'd have to give part of the payoff to the rock surgeon, but he'd pocket the rest. Easy money.

It was then that he heard the sound.

"You hear that?" he demanded.

Ryan looked up, the blade of his tool glinting in the lamplight. "Hear what? Hey, the Hodags got you spooked? You know, we're pretty deep in the belly of the cave, all alone in the bowels of the Earth. Legend has it that when the Hodags slither out from their hiding places to—"

"Just shut up and get back to work," the man snapped. *"I'll tell you one thing—I learned a long time ago to make sure there ain't no witnesses. If a Hodag-thing is down here, watchin' what we're doing, I'll kill him dead."*

"Yeah. I'm sure you would." Ryan just shook his head.

CHAPTER ONE

"I can't wait! How much longer until it happens?" Ashley asked, squinting into the desert sky streaked orange by the setting sun. In front of them, the cave entrance loomed large and dark, like a gigantic, yawning mouth. Jack tried not to notice the pungent odor that wafted from Carlsbad Cavern and concentrated instead on adjusting his camera lens, focusing in, then out. Hundreds of park visitors were seated in the stone amphitheater, watching, pointing, waiting for the first wave of bats to spiral out of the entrance. Shifting to get a better view, Jack snapped a picture of cactus that seemed to bubble up from the rock itself. Perfect. With the play between light and shadow, he knew he could get some real quality shots.

"Hey, save some film for the bat flight," his sister, Ashley, told him.

"I will. I've got another roll."

"Aren't you excited for them to come out? 'Cause you don't look too excited."

"I'm excited," Jack answered, zooming in on a

rock squirrel.

Leaning back on her elbows, Ashley cocked her head and gave him a knowing look. The amphitheater benches were deep, almost three feet of stone and concrete still warm from baking in the day's sun. With her head tilted that way, Ashley's dark braids curled like question marks. "Come on, Jack, admit it. No matter what the rangers say, you're still afraid of bats. You think the bats'll suck your blood and leave you shriveled up like a raisin." Pointing a finger, she said, "Remember how you used to try to scare me every time we went camping? You'd say bats always go for girls with long, curly hair. But it was really you who was scared."

"No way!" Jack snorted. Now that she was 11, Ashley had a little more attitude, but, being two years older, Jack could handle it. Turning to their newest temporary foster child, Jack said, "Sammy, you've got to ignore all this blood-sucking stuff. You heard the ranger. The only blood-sucking bats live far, far away from here. The ones in Carlsbad are Mexican free-tailed bats. Free-tailed bats eat tons of bugs, so they're good bats," Jack declared. "And I was never afraid of any bats."

"Liar," Ashley laughed. "So who do you think is telling the truth, Sammy? Me, or my mean brother, who used to terrify me with spooky stories when he was really the one who was scared?"

Ducking his round, blond head, Sam whispered, "I

d-d-don't know." He began to fidget with the end of his dirty shoelace so that, Jack guessed, he wouldn't have to look at either one of them. Although he'd been with their family for three weeks, Sam still didn't know the Landons well enough to understand the way Jack and Ashley teased. Well, from what Ms. Lopez, Sam's social worker, had told them, there hadn't been much in the boy's life to laugh about. That was why Jack's mother and father were glad Sam could go with them all the way to New Mexico to see the magnificent cavern of Carlsbad. "If anyone deserves a break," Jack's father, Steven, had said, "it's this kid."

Jack looked up to see a watery moon appear like a ghost in the sky, faint and silvery in the twilight. The clouds seemed to blaze even brighter as the last rays of sun set them on fire. If the bats flew out soon, Jack would have a perfect canvas to frame them. Focusing his lens, he snapped a picture of the clouds, double-checking that his flash was off. The ranger had instructed all of the visitors to turn off their camera flash attachments, since the sound from a flash—even though humans didn't notice it—might throw off the bats' sensitive navigation system.

Barely tapping his shoe with the edge of his worn sneaker, Sam looked at Jack with large eyes. His hair was clipped ragged, as if he'd trimmed it himself. But what kind of eight-year-old would cut his own hair? Not anyone who lived in the Landons' Jackson Hole neighborhood, where all the kids had their own bikes and computers and enough money in their pockets to buy fast food whenever they wanted. Although Sam hadn't told them much about his life, Jack could tell he came from a different world, a world Jack was glad he didn't live in.

"So J-Jack, you're not really s-c-c-ared? Of the b-b-bats?"

"Nah. Ashley and me, we're just kidding around. Don't take us seriously."

"OK. I'm not s-s-scared, either."

Mmmm, maybe not of the bats, Jack thought. But ever since they'd had him, Sam had seemed, if not frightened, at least nervous all the time. Did some unknown fear make Sam stutter the way he did? The poor kid couldn't get out two words without stuttering. Sometimes he'd start to say something and then just give up, as though whatever he'd wanted to say simply wasn't worth the struggle to force it out. Ms. Lopez had said that although Sam's school grades were poor because of his stuttering problem, inside he was really a bright little boy.

Just then Ashley grabbed Jack's arm and pointed excitedly at a small black object streaking by. "Is that one? Quick—take a picture! It's right there—see?"

"Duh. That's a cave swallow," Jack replied. "It has a beak. Bird—beak. Bat—ugly gargoyle face. Get the difference?"

"If you call them ugly, they'll hear you and stay there in the cave all night and they'll never come out," she declared.

"Honest?" Sam worried.

Jack assured him, "No, Sammy, Ashley was only

joking again."

"But we've been waiting an awful long time," Ashley said, sighing. "Mom, do you think they're ever going to come out of the cave?"

"Hmm?" their mother, Olivia, murmured, barely looking up from a stack of papers. A yellow highlighter was poised in her hand, and every few minutes she underlined a sentence or bracketed a paragraph until the paper seemed to glow neon. A wildlife veterinarian, Olivia Landon had come to New Mexico to study the decline in the number of bats occupying Carlsbad Cavern. Mountains of scientific papers had been faxed to her before they'd left their home in Wyoming, which meant that for the entire trip on the plane, she'd been nose-deep in study. Jack had never seen her read so much so furiously.

"Earth to Mom," Ashley cried, cupping her hands around her mouth. "You're the expert. Do bats ever stay inside the cavern and just skip a night? Because I think that might be what they're doing here."

Looking up, Olivia blinked. "Skip? Oh, no. Don't worry, sweetheart, they'll fly. You just have to be patient. Remember, bats are wild animals, not a circus act trained to appear on cue." Taking off her reading glasses, Olivia rubbed the bridge of her nose. "What makes them swarm is one of the great bat mysteries. Even the latest research—" she tapped her glasses onto the paper—"even this can't explain why they fly out the way they do or why they choose the particular moment they decide to emerge."

Olivia's dark, curly hair had been pushed up under a baseball cap, although strands escaped in tendrils that wound past her shoulders. Her hiking boots, scarred from years of climbing over rough terrain, were the same tan as her legs. Ashley was a smaller version of Olivia, with the identical olive skin that just grew darker throughout the summer. It was Jack and his father who had to slather on sunscreen or risk burning to a crisp. Jack, Steven, and now Sam, who shared their fair coloring.

"By the way," Olivia said, "can any of you kids see where your dad's gone off to?"

Scanning the crowd, Jack looked for a tall, blond head, but it was useless. So many people had crowded together on the benches that it seemed as though a giant handful of confetti had been tossed into the amphitheater. He was about to say that there was no way anyone could spot anyone in that place when Sammy announced, "He's over th-there, with that r-ranger."

"Way to go, Sammy! Could you go get him for me?" Olivia asked. "He's not too far from here. I'll watch you the whole time."

Sam shook his head no.

"OK, how about if Ashley goes with you. Would that be all right?"

Without answering, Sam nodded. Following Ashley, he made his way toward the ramp, his sturdy legs pumping hard to stay right behind Ashley as he climbed the stone steps.

"At least Sam went with Ashley," Olivia said to Jack. "He's becoming far too dependent on you, Jack."

"Hey, Sam's OK," Jack countered. "He's doing better."

"Better with you," Olivia reminded him. "Not better with your dad or Ashley or me. You're the only one out of all of us he feels really safe with."

That much was true, and all of the Landons knew it. When Ms. Lopez had arrived with Sam, he'd clung to her, big-eyed and silent.

"Sam, remember what we talked about," Ms. Lopez had said in her gentlest voice. "Since your mother is so sick, the Landons are going to take care of you, just until your own mom gets better."

"Hi, Sam," Olivia had said. Bending down to eye level, she'd reached out her hand, but Sam had shrunk back behind Ms. Lopez's green dress until only half of his body could be seen. Ms. Lopez shot them all a concerned look as she gently pulled Sam forward, saying, "This is Steven. And this is Ashley." Sam tried to slip behind her again, but she held him firm, her scarlet nails pressed into his shoulders. "Now I want you to meet Jack. My, would you look at that!" Ms. Lopez broke into a warm smile. "Do you see it? You two could pass for brothers. Same blond hair and blue eyes, and the same chin. An amazing resemblance, don't you think?"

Since Jack didn't know what to do, he said the first lame thing that popped into his mind. "Yeah, I guess we do look alike. So Sam, how 'bout if I call you Mini-Me." He could hardly believe it when the barest smile crept across Sam's face. The boy's lids had fluttered up, revealing light blue eyes the color of a robin's egg. He really was cute, with his pale blond hair and moon-shaped face. Encouraged, Jack said, "Hey, Sam, I was in the Everglades a while back, and I shot a picture of an alligator eating a turtle. Would you like to see it?"

It took a moment for Sam to respond. Finally, he gave a slight nod, edging to the front of Ms. Lopez.

"Jack," Olivia broke in, flashing him a look, "maybe that picture isn't the right one to show him. It's a little…graphic."

Jack was about to answer when Sam gave a tortured, "I don't c-c-care. I want to see the t-t-turtle."

Although they'd been warned Sam was a stutterer, Jack wasn't prepared for how hard Sam had to work to get those words past his lips. Sam's whole face flushed as he looked back at the floor, the color deepening as it spread down his neck like a red stain. Pretending that he didn't notice, Jack said, "Tell you what, I'll show you my camera and teach you how it works."

"You m-m-mean I can try the c-c-camera?"

"Sure. Just don't break it or anything."

That had been the start. And now, three weeks later,

Sam seemed to be more attached to Jack than ever. He followed Jack's every move, as if the two of them were pedals on a bike that worked in tandem. And Jack didn't really mind. It was nice finding out what it would have been like to have a brother. Although having a sister was fine, a brother definitely would have been different. Sam had dived into the box of Tonka trucks Jack kept in the back of his closet for old times' sake; he never got tired of shuffling through Jack's football cards or leafing through Jack's photography magazines; and he seemed fascinated by Jack's pictures, taking a roll of passable shots of his own. Although he didn't say much, Jack could tell how much Sam liked him. There were worse things than sharing a house with this kid.

Now, as Sam and Steven and Ashley returned to their seats, Jack realized the crowd was buzzing. Somewhere behind them a cell phone played a tune but was quickly silenced as the anticipation grew. And then, as suddenly as a puff of smoke, the first bats emerged to a loud *ooohhhh* from the crowd. They spiraled out of the cavern's mouth, past its rock lip and up into the sky like a whirling coil. Sam watched wide-eyed, his neck rolled back, his mouth slightly ajar, fists clenched.

"You OK?" Jack asked, wondering if the bats might scare Sam.

"Uh-huh. Are y-you?"

"Who, me? Yeah, sure. Of course." Why did Sam ask

that? Jack knew that he was quite safe as the creatures streaked overhead like tiny black missiles, guided by their perfect sonar system. They were not going to land in anyone's hair—that was only a myth.

Never would he admit it to Ashley, but something deep inside Jack chilled at the thought of what was erupting from the cave's inky blackness. That explosion of almost half a million swarming bats, hundreds of thousands of bizarre-looking creatures mushrooming from the depths of that enormous cavern, really did make his pulse rate rise. Jack pictured what it would be like to descend into one of the smaller caves in the vast network of Carlsbad Caverns. The Big Room wouldn't bother him, he knew that, not with its gigantic spaces and spectacular formations and columns. But the thought of some of those smaller, tighter, more confined spaces, dark as pitch and bristling with bats, made the hair on the back of his neck stand up.

Sam had seen a map of the hidden rooms that snaked though the cavern, and in his halting way he'd begged Jack to take him on the deeper trails, one called Left Hand Tunnel. Well, it couldn't happen before tomorrow, so there was no use worrying about it now. But how could Jack explain to an eight-year-old that the idea of a narrow, deep, dark tunnel full of bats left Jack less than enthusiastic? Sam's life had already spooked him enough as it was. No, let him believe Jack wasn't afraid of anything. He didn't need Jack's fears to add to his own pile.

More bats began to wheel up and out in a clockwise formation until it looked as though a column of smoke rose from an abyss. They came in bursts of black, fits and starts of bats, hundreds of them, thousands of them. In the dusk, he could see Sam watching, riveted and fascinated. Jack shook his head in amazement. After three weeks with the Landons, Sam still wouldn't say ten words to Olivia or Steven or Ashley, and yet, when faced with bats and caves, he didn't act scared at all. Only people seemed to frighten him.

"I want to g-go in there. T-t-tomorrow. You're g-going to t-take me, right?"

"To the Big Room? Sure. That's the most famous room in the cavern. You'll really like it."

"No. Not th-there."

"Why not?" Jack protested. "Sammy, come on, the Big Room's really cool!"

Sam shook his head slowly, stubbornly, and said, "No. The tunnel."

What was it about the tunnel? What made Sam want to crawl into a narrow, dark place beneath the earth? As more bats whizzed overhead, Jack thought back over the few facts his parents had shared about Sam's life. He lived in a rough neighborhood an hour's drive from Jackson Hole. His father was a mystery—the Landons didn't know what had happened to him, except that he was gone from Sammy's life. His mother had overdosed on drugs and was now in jail, and Sam had no other relative to take him.

The kid had faced a lot and asked for little. Jack had a lot and asked for more. When he thought about it, he knew there was no way he could turn down Sammy's request. Anyway, Jack was Sammy's hero, and a hero shouldn't look like a wimp.

No longer hesitating, Jack answered, "OK, Mini-Me, let's do it. Tomorrow. If it's OK with Mom and Dad and Ashley."

Sam didn't say a word. In the dim light, Jack could see him smile.

CHAPTER TWO

"Come on, kids," Steven said. "Get moving, or we'll be late for our appointment with the bat woman."

"B-b-bat woman?" Sam asked. "Like in the movies?" When Jack burst out laughing, Ashley gave a sharp yank on his arm and pulled him back to whisper in his ear, "Stop that! Sammy will think you're laughing at his stammer."

"I'm not!" Jack protested, but Ashley only hissed at him, "Show some sensitivity!"

"OK." Making sure his expression was serious, Jack leaned down to tell Sam, "There's no Bat Woman in the movies. There's Batman and Batgirl and Catwoman, but no Bat Woman. What my dad meant was that we're going to see a naturalist who knows everything about bats, and she happens to be a woman."

"That's right," Olivia added, "and you kids are really lucky to get to meet Dr. Rhodes. She's a world-renowned expert on bats."

Ashley sighed and said, "I know we're lucky, and I really want to hear all about bats, but when do we get to go inside the cavern? I thought we were supposed to do that this morning."

They'd reached the bottom of some stairs that led to the door of a building made of limestone blocks. Peering through the window glass in the front door, Olivia answered, "Your dad will take you there after we see the bat woman—whoops!" Blushing, she said, "Now you've got me doing it, Sammy. I hope I don't call her that by mistake—it would be an embarrassing way to meet her. Anyway, after you kids and your dad leave Dr. Rhodes's office, I'll stay with her to learn more about the bats."

"So let's get started," Steven suggested, leaning across Olivia to push the door wide. While he held it open, the three short ones—Olivia, Ashley, and Sam walked under Steven's extended arm into the corridor. Jack was now too tall to fit under his father's arm, and he liked that. With every inch he grew, he felt a bit more grown-up. He figured that one of these years he might actually outgrow his father, who was nearly six feet four.

"Come in, come in!" Dr. Rhodes welcomed them. For a world expert, she had a small office, Jack thought, and only three chairs.

"The kids can sit on the floor," Steven quickly offered. "These two are our kids—Jack and Ashley—and Sam Sexton is our guest."

Guest. That was the word the Landons liked to use for the short-term foster kids who stayed with them from time to time, kids who needed a safe place to live until their problems could be solved.

"Pleased to m-meet you," Sam said, hardly stuttering as he took the hand Dr. Rhodes held out to him.

"How are you, Sam?" Smiling warmly, Dr. Rhodes told him, "You sit here, closest to my chair, so you'll have the best look at the pictures I'm going to show everyone." Jack wondered whether his mother had clued Dr. Rhodes in on Sam's background. Or maybe Dr. Rhodes was just naturally nice to small kids.

"Well," she said, "let's start. Your mom said you wanted to hear about bats. The first things I'm going to tell you are what bats are not!" She laughed a little, then went on, "They're not birds, and they're not blind, although they are color-blind. They don't get tangled in people's hair, and they don't suck blood—well, actually, three species do drink blood, but those species don't live anywhere near here."

Ashley's hand flew to her neck. "Where do they live?" she asked quickly.

"In our hemisphere, they're in Mexico, Central America, and South America. But less than one percent of the world's bats are vampire bats, and two of the vampire bat species feed only on birds. The third species prefers mammals, but Ashley, you don't have to worry about your neck. They're more likely to go after your toes."

Sammy's eyes had grown wide.

"Nothing to be afraid of, Sam," Dr. Rhodes told him.

"The Mexican free-tailed bats, the kind we mostly have around here, eat only bugs." She held up a picture of a brown, fuzzy bat with hooded eyes, rounded ears, and wings folded like fans. "They're wonderful animals. To me, they look like little gnomes. They're mammals, you know, which means the mothers nurse their pups— that's what the babies are called. Pups. Did you know that?"

All three kids shook their heads. "So now there are three animals I know of that have pups," Ashley announced. "Dogs, wolves, and bats. I learned about the wolves in Yellowstone National Park."

Jack got a mental image of a gnomelike mamma bat with her wings wrapped around a little gnome-faced pup. "How do the mothers hold them?" he asked. "I mean, they hang upside down, don't they? How do they keep from dropping the pups?"

Dr. Rhodes answered, "It's the babies that hold on to the mother, with their feet and their thumbs and their tiny teeth. Like you kids, little bats lose their baby teeth after a while and get grown-up teeth. When the mothers leave to get their nightly meal of insects, the baby bats hang by their toes on the walls and ceilings of the caves, packed so tightly together that there can be 400 of them in a one-square-foot area. Think of that." Dr. Rhodes opened her desk drawer and took out a ruler. "Twelve inches on each side of a square, and 400 bat babies all squeezed together into that little space. That closeness keeps them warm, because a cave is kind of cold." She threw the ruler back into the drawer, then held up another photo that showed bats clustered together so tightly they looked like ink blots on a gray cave ceiling.

"Wow!" Ashley exclaimed. "How do the mothers ever find their babies in all that crowd?"

"Good question, Ashley. By smell and by sound. Even though a hundred thousand pups get born in the spring, a mother can pick out her own infant—she has only one baby a year. Both mother and pup make these high-pitched sounds that people can't hear but the bats can. It guides them to each other. That same high-frequency echolocation guides them when they go outside the cave, too. It tells them where the insects are."

Dr. Rhodes winced a little, then reached down to pick up an empty wastebasket. After she turned it upside down, she carefully placed her left foot on top of it. An elastic bandage had been wrapped around her ankle. "A sprain," she explained when she saw the Landons looking at it. "I tried to take a shortcut down a slippery slope, and I twisted my ankle."

"Does it hurt?" Olivia asked. "Yes, of course it must hurt. The kids shouldn't be taking up any more of your time, Dr. Rhodes."

"Oh, it doesn't hurt me that much," she answered. "It's fun to talk to kids; I enjoy it. Anyway, I'll just end this little session with a few more bat facts. Like this one—bats'

knees bend backward, not forward like yours." She pointed
to Sam, whose knees were tucked under his chin. Ashley
looked thoughtfully at her own knees, probably wondering
how it would feel if they bent backward.

"And bats have been around for 50 million years,"
Dr. Rhodes went on. "We know that from finding fossils that
old. But most of all, I want you to remember that
bats are intelligent creatures and tremendously useful
ecologically. If there are 400,000 bats flying out of Carlsbad
Cavern every night eating bugs, can you imagine how many
tons of bugs that makes in a month? In a year?
That's a tremendous help to farmers."

"How much can each bat eat?" Jack asked.

"Considering the size of a bat, quite a lot. A nursing
female will leave her baby tucked nice and warm with
the other pups in the 'bat nursery,' then fly out into the
night to eat her entire body weight—about 12 or 13
grams—in insects. Then she'll return to her baby, nurse
it again, and maybe fly out a second time in a single night
to eat that many bugs all over again. Then back to her
baby. She never leaves her baby for long. She's a gentle,
caring mother."

Sam, who'd seemed fascinated by Dr. Rhodes's
lesson, suddenly looked as though he were about to cry.
Maybe it was the mention of "a gentle, caring mother,"
which Sam didn't have. Steven must have noticed Sam's
sad expression too, because he stood up and said, "I guess

we'd better get going. I told the kids I'd take them into the cavern. Sammy's really anxious to see Left Hand Tunnel."

"Left Hand Tunnel? Two different species of bats live there," Dr. Rhodes said, "the cave myotis and the fringed myotis. Both species are quite rare. We've counted only 354 of the cave myotis and only 12 of the fringed myotis."

Well, Jack thought, at least that particular tunnel wouldn't be teeming with countless thousands of bats. He felt a little relieved.

"I hope I get to see those rare bats," Steven told her. "I'm really anxious to shoot some pictures like the ones you just showed us."

"Steven is a photographer," Olivia explained.

"Oh." Dr. Rhodes hesitated, then said, "Well, you understand, Mr. Landon, that you'll have to use infrared film in the caves."

"Uh…no! I knew I couldn't use the flash attachment when the bats were flying out of the cavern because it interferes with their echolocation system—their sonar. But I figured that when they weren't flying, when they're just hanging in the caves, I could use my regular flash attachment with fast film."

"Uh-uh." Dr. Rhodes shook her head. "The light from a flash attachment, or any kind of light at all, really bothers the bats. That's why we keep the lighting in the Big Room quite low, and in Left Hand Tunnel there's no light at all. You'll have to use infrared film and an infrared filter on your flash."

Steven looked crestfallen. "I don't have any of that with me. But—do you think I can buy these things in the city of Carlsbad? Would a photo store carry them?"

"I'm sure it would."

"Then I'll just have to drive back to Carlsbad," Steven said. "Right now."

"Da-ad!" Ashley complained, drawing it out into two syllables. "I thought you were going to take us through the cavern."

"Left Hand T-T-Tunnel," Sammy agreed, nodding.

Carefully, favoring her sore ankle, Dr. Rhodes got to her feet before she told them, "Your dad couldn't take you through Left Hand Tunnel by himself—you have to sign up to be part of a tour group. Let's see, what time is it? You might be able to hook up with a tour, but you'll need an adult with you. Kids under 16 aren't allowed to tour the cavern without a parent or guardian."

All their plans seemed to be falling apart, Jack realized. Their dad wanted to make the long drive back to the city of Carlsbad. It would take him at least two hours to get there, find a store, buy the film and filter—if the store had them— and drive back. Their mother needed to stay with Dr. Rhodes. Ashley and Sam and Jack couldn't tour the cavern without an adult. So what were they supposed to do?

"I have an idea," Dr. Rhodes said. "I can take you kids down into the cavern and see if there's still room in the next tour to Left Hand Tunnel. I know the ranger who's guiding the tour, so even if it's pretty full, she might bend the rules a little bit and let you join the group as her responsibility."

"Dr. Rhodes, I can't let you make that trip down into the cavern," Olivia objected. "I can see that you're in pain from that swollen ankle."

Wavering between hope and disappointment, Sam's big eyes kept traveling from one adult to another. Ashley, too, seemed to be holding her breath, waiting to see how it would all turn out.

"Here's another thought," Dr. Rhodes said. "I'll ask one of the office assistants to take the kids down. We'll pull a little rank and get them into that tour."

Ashley clapped her hands, which made her look like she was as young as Sam. Was Jack the only one who wasn't all hot to go through those narrow, dark tunnels? He'd better not show it, or Ashley would make some smart-faced remark.

When they exited Dr. Rhodes's office, they found only one woman seated at a desk, typing fast on a computer.

"Hello, Consuela. Where are the others?" Dr. Rhodes asked her.

"They've all gone to lunch. I wanted to finish this report, so I told them to go ahead without me." Consuela was a pretty woman, round and soft with big brown eyes and black hair pulled into a ponytail. "Can I help you?"

she asked.

After Dr. Rhodes introduced them all and explained the situation, Consuela said, "I can take the kids down to the cavern. I'm just finishing this report now."

"Great!" Steven exclaimed, pulling out his wallet. "This is to pay for the tour. And there's a lunchroom down in the cavern, right? Here's some extra money so the kids can buy themselves lunch, and you, too, Ms...uh...."

"Sandoval. Consuela Sandoval. But call me Consuela. Thanks, Mr. Landon. I'll get everybody fed before the tour departs. It's a great tour. My grandson loves it."

"You have grandkids?" Olivia blurted. "You look way too young."

Consuela grinned and said, "I was married at 16, and I have two grown sons plus a 9-year-old grandson, but thanks for the compliment." Turning to the three kids, she said, "We'd better get started. Do you all have something warm to wear? Most of the caves are just 56 degrees, although parts of Left Hand Tunnel are warmer than that. Still, it can feel pretty chilly when you're there for a while."

Jack and Ashley opened their backpacks and took out fleecy hooded sweatshirts; Jack's was blue, Ashley's gray. Sam had a mustard-colored fake-leather zippered jacket. It was too small, but at least it would keep him warm.

"We're good to go," Ashley announced. "See you later, Mom and Dad."

CHAPTER THREE

Outside the visitor center, the temperature had risen to 100 degrees; on the walk from Dr. Rhodes's office, Jack had to wipe sweat from his forehead. It was hard to believe that when they descended into the cavern, they'd feel chilly.

"How do we get down to the cavern?" Ashley asked.

"Well," Consuela answered, "if we had more time, we'd go to the natural entrance of the cave and hike down the twisty, turny path to the bottom. But that would take about an hour, and you'd miss your tour. So we'll use the elevator."

"Elevator?" That was a surprise to Jack. In all the national parks his family had visited, they'd never reached a natural wonder by elevator. That sounded kind of out of line with National Park policy, which was to keep everything exactly as it was in nature.

"Just wait till you try it," Consuela told them. "It's quite a ride."

They'd entered the visitor center, filled with hundreds of tourists from all over the globe who were milling around, strolling from the gift shop to the bookstore to the restaurant and all the other attractions in between. There were exhibits on bats, geology, and the history of Carlsbad Caverns, plus movies that showed how the formations grew. "I want to check out all this stuff after we tour the cavern," Jack told Ashley, and Consuela added, "You can spend hours in here and not see everything. And then there are the trails outside. They're worth checking out, too."

Little kids of all shades ran around the center, shouting to each other in different languages. Since it happened to be late July, school was no longer in session. Older kids studied the exhibits.

"Elevator's over this way," Consuela said, leading them. She reached for Sam's hand so he wouldn't get swept away in the throng of visitors. He smiled up at her shyly as they came to a stop in front of the elevator doors. At least for a little while, Sam was holding on to someone other than Jack, and Jack enjoyed the freedom.

Soon the elevator doors opened, and the four of them entered. "Now, hold on to your sombreros," Consuela said. "We're about to descend 754 feet in less than a minute. See that little box up there? Watch the numbers, and it'll show you how fast we're going down." The doors closed, the elevator began to drop, and Jack's stomach lurched.

He grabbed on to the elevator wall, afraid he'd get queasy, but the ride was surprisingly smooth. He couldn't take his eyes off the red digital numbers that measured their fall: 50 feet, 100 feet, 200—the red numbers changed with every 50 feet the elevator dropped—250, 350, 500, 650, 700—wow! What a ride! It was almost like free-falling in outer space. All too soon they reached ground zero, where Consuela said, "End of the trip. Everybody out!"

They exited into an incredible scene. There they were, 754 feet beneath the surface of the Earth in a big, dark cavern—and straight ahead of them was a gift shop! On display were T-shirts with Carlsbad Caverns printed across the front and all kinds of other Carlsbad souvenirs. Beyond that was a photo-supply shop, then a kiosk selling food, and lots of picnic tables, all of them hardly visible in this barely lighted subterranean chamber. The usual crowd of visitors wandered around, calling their kids in half a dozen languages.

"This is the cavern?" Ashley asked. "It looks like Disneyland, only darker."

Consuela just smiled. "This is only the starting point," she said. "The cavern and caves and tunnels snake out for 30 miles beyond here—at least that's how much has been discovered so far. Let's go! We need to eat quickly if you're going to make that two o'clock tour."

Jack and Ashley ordered slices of pizza; Consuela ordered chicken strips; and Sam said all he wanted was one of the big soft pretzels. "That's not enough," Jack told him. "Do you want to keep on being a Mini-Me, or do you want to grow up nice and tall like I am?" At that, Sam agreed to order a hot dog.

"And milk," Jack told him. "Milk will help you grow."

"G-g-get some for Ashley, then," Sam said, which made Jack laugh loudly until Ashley stuck her tongue out at him.

They found an empty picnic table littered with crumpled napkins and discarded cups. Consuela quickly swept them up and deposited the trash into a nearby garbage bin, clucking, "Honestly, people should be more careful. This is a national park, after all!"

When they finally settled in, the smooth plastic benches felt cold beneath Jack's jeans. He was just taking a bite of pizza when Consuela asked, "Kids, would you mind getting some utensils? I could never eat chicken with just my fingers, even if most people do. I'll need a plastic knife and fork."

"Sure," Jack agreed, getting up.

"Ashley, you and Sam go, too," Consuela said.

"Huh?" Ashley's pizza stopped in midair, just inches from her lips.

"You all go. And get me some"—Consuela's dark eyes seemed to search the kiosk—"some napkins. And an extra cup. And some salt and pepper, too. And honey if they have some. Please."

"But Jack can—" Ashley began.

"Don't leave your brother to do it all. Go on, now," Consuela told them, making a shooing gesture with her hands. "Take Sam with you."

Giving Jack a look, Ashley shrugged and said, "OK. Let's go, Sam."

Without a word, Sam slid out from the bench and trotted after Jack and Ashley.

The whole thing struck Jack as odd. The kiosk was only 40 feet away, yet Consuela was asking three kids to do the work of one. Whatever! he told himself as he began to gather up the plastic supplies she'd requested. The extra cup would take a little longer, since they'd have to wait in line for that. Ashley had unfolded a paper napkin to hold the various packages of condiments.

"I'll t-t-take the f-f-fork," Sam offered. "She c-c-can start eating."

"You do that, Mini-Me," Jack answered. "We'll be right behind you."

"Jeez, I hope my pizza won't be stone cold," Ashley murmured as she dropped three packets of salt into the makeshift bag. "I still don't know why all three of us had to get this stuff."

"Who knows? Maybe Consuela believes in teamwork or something," Jack guessed.

When they finally set the napkin full of condiments in front of Consuela, her skin had flushed to the color of copper. "Thanks a lot, kids. Now, you'd better hurry up and eat. Sam here says he's not hungry, but I've never met a boy who couldn't pack in enough for three adults. Maybe you can get him to take a bite. He's just been fiddling with that pretzel."

Right away, Jack noticed there was something

wrong with Sam. It was as if in their absence the air had been sucked out of him. His eyes were glued to the tabletop, and he had shrunk into himself the way he'd done when he'd first arrived at the Landon home. Only the pretzel moved, swinging back and forth between his fingers like the pendulum on a clock.

"Hey, what's wrong, guy?" Jack asked, sliding next to him.

Pressing his lips together, Sam quickly dropped the pretzel onto the tabletop and turned away, his shoulder blades protruding like knives.

"I think I know what may have upset him," Consuela began, but just then a man at an adjoining table said something to her in Spanish.

"Que es?" she answered. Since she was wearing a park uniform, the man must have thought she was a park ranger rather than an office worker. He spoke rapidly to her, interrupted by his wife, who kept breaking in with comments of her own, all in Spanish. Every time Consuela tried to take a bite of her food, they stopped her with another question, which she politely answered. Both the husband and wife took turns speaking excitedly in a stream of nonstop Spanish, which kept up the whole time Ashley, Jack, and Sam were eating their lunches. Poor Consuela never got a mouthful.

Whatever she had been about to say about Sam and his strange behavior seemed to get lost as she focused on the man, who gestured wildly at the cave ceiling as if he could punch it with his fists. Although Jack didn't understand Spanish, there was one word he could make out—"no." Whatever the man was saying, Consuela was arguing against.

For some reason, Sam had shrunk to the end of the bench, pressing himself close to Jack as though he were trying to get as far away as possible from Consuela.

"Hey, move over," Jack told him. "You're crowding me."

Sam moved about an inch, then slid down on the bench until his chin almost touched the tabletop. What is with this kid? Jack wondered impatiently. He was about to ask when Consuela tapped the face of her wristwatch, apparently telling the Hispanic couple that she had to go, because at the same time she got up and gestured to the kids. She looked regretfully at her uneaten chicken strips, then took them over to the trash bin with all the rest of the debris from the table, saying, "We have to move or you'll miss the tour. The last one of the day will start in ten minutes."

"You know, if we miss it, we don't have to tour Left Hand Tunnel," Ashley suggested. "We could just walk through the Big Room. That's a self-guided tour, isn't it?"

"Nuh-uh!" Sam insisted. "L-Left Hand Tunnel."

"Why?" Ashley demanded. "That's all you've talked about ever since we got here. What is so important about Left Hand Tunnel?"

"B-because." Sam took a deep breath and managed to

get the whole sentence out without stammering. "It's about people like me."

"You mean stutterers?" Ashley asked uncertainly.

"No." Sam looked disdainful as he raised his hand and wiggled his fingers. "L-l-lefties. Southpaws." He pretended to throw an imaginary baseball with his left hand.

Consuela, Jack, and Ashley were so surprised that for a moment none of them could think of anything to say. Then Consuela murmured, "That's a great reason to visit Left Hand Tunnel. I'll go check with the ranger."

Should Jack explain to Sam that the tunnel wasn't named for left-handed people? Or just let him go on thinking that it had been? Sometimes Sam seemed a whole lot younger than his eight years. Like now, when once more he kept clinging to Jack's arm.

"Hey, what's with you?" Jack asked him. "Why are you hanging on me like a leech? Are you afraid of this place because it's dark?"

Sam shook his head, and motioned for Jack to lean down so he could whisper. When Jack did, Sam muttered, "She's on d-d-drugs."

"Your mother?" Jack answered. "Yes, I know that, and I'm sorry."

But Sammy shook his head. "No. C-C-C—" Unable to finish the word, he just pointed to Consuela's retreating figure.

"Consuela?" Jack exclaimed. "Don't be crazy."

"I saw!" Sam insisted. Finding it easier to pantomime

than speak, he went through the motions of injecting his arm with a needle, then pointed again to Consuela.

"What's he saying?" Ashley asked.

"He's trying to tell us he saw Consuela shooting up with heroin or something."

"Oh, Sammy, that's insane," Ashley declared, also bending down to his eye level. "Consuela's a nice lady with a grandson about your age. She's no druggie. I'm sure it must be hard on you to know that your mother takes drugs, but you can't go around thinking that every other woman you meet does the same thing. Consuela's really sweet. Didn't you notice how nice she was to those Hispanic people who wouldn't even let her eat her lunch?"

"She did it b-b-before that. When you were getting the s-s-stuff. I saw!"

"Well, I didn't see anything." Jack said.

"Neither did I. You're just plain wrong, Sammy," Ashley insisted, and to Jack, "Don't say anything about this to Consuela. Can you imagine how she'd feel? That would be so insulting."

"Do you think I'd say anything? No way. Anyhow, she's coming back right now."

"I'm so sorry," Consuela apologized. "My watch was slow, and we missed the start of the tour. We're about five minutes late. They're going to let us in anyway, but we'll have to wait for another one of the rangers to come down from the visitor center and unlock the door to Left Hand Tunnel. It's kept locked at all times except to let the tour groups in and out."

"It was those people who made us late," Ashley complained. "The ones who kept talking and talking to you and wouldn't even let you eat your chicken strips. What was all that about?"

"Oh, they just wanted to tell me the latest news about the *Chupacabras.*"

"The Chew—pa—" Ashley tried unsuccessfully to repeat it, mangling the word worse than Sam would have. "What're they?"

"Also known as the Goatsuckers. They're monsters that are supposed to be three feet tall with big ears and wide, folded wings like bats, with fangs and claws and spikes down their backs. And they suck blood. At least that's what the rumors say. People from Puerto Rico to Tijuana to Texas and even as far as Oregon claim to have seen them."

Dr. Rhodes's words came back to Jack. "Are you talking about vampire bats?" he asked, incredulous.

Consuela shook her head. "My boss, Dr. Rhodes, would get upset if she heard me even repeat what those people said. But lots of people say they've seen Chupacabras. They call them vampire bats, but you know, actual vampire bats are quite small. Tiny, even. The people who believe in Chupacabras describe them as huge. Some think they might be genetic experiments that escaped from a laboratory. Or even creatures from outer space. Aliens."

"But you don't believe anything like that, do you?" Ashley pressed.

"Of course not." But for a few seconds, Consuela hesitated. "Still…my cousin in Juarez, Mexico, wrote to me that three of her goats were killed one night, with puncture wounds in their necks and all the blood sucked out of them. And those people talking to me at lunch—they were from Arecibo in Puerto Rico—they said at a village near Arecibo, 34 hogs were killed by a Chupacabra in just one night."

When Consuela saw the concern growing in Sam's eyes, she quickly added, "But it's all just fairy tales. People will believe in all kinds of imaginary things, like Bigfoot or the aliens that were supposed to have landed at Roswell, New Mexico. Did you know that Roswell is not all that far from here?"

Jack had begun to worry about Sam. First the boy had thought he'd seen Consuela taking drugs. Now he was hearing stories about the Chupacabras, the Goatsuckers who supposedly sucked the blood out of farm animals. No wonder Sammy was clinging so tightly to Jack's arm that it hurt. Even Ashley looked a little nervous.

"I'm going to call upstairs again to make sure the ranger's coming to unlock the door for us," Consuela was saying. "You kids wait here. I'll be right back."

"Wow!" Ashley breathed. "You know, Jack, those

people who were talking to Consuela about the Chupacabras didn't look like weirdos or anything. They looked like perfectly normal people. What if they were telling the truth? Vampire bats—oooh—yuck!"

"Don't be silly," Jack told her, moving a little behind Sammy and pointing down at him with his free hand, trying to give Ashley the message that she shouldn't scare Sam over a fairy tale. "People make up all kinds of stories all the time. They see movies or television shows about monsters and they start to think they're real. But they're not real! There's no such thing as vampire bats three feet tall with spikes down their backs."

"Oh, sure, you're right," Ashley agreed, getting the message. "No such thing as aliens, either. But, Jack—did you realize Roswell was near Carlsbad? I mean—I saw it on TV about aliens landing in Roswell. But I know that isn't true," she added hastily.

Consuela came toward them, carrying two old-fashioned looking lanterns, one in each hand. Ten inches tall, they were made of wooden posts with glass panels between the posts, and handles above. Inside each lantern was a thick, white candle, unlit.

"What's with the lanterns?" Ashley asked.

"Oh, there's no light in Left Hand Tunnel. It's completely dark. Everyone is supposed to carry a lantern, but there were only two left, so Jack can have one and I'll carry the other."

"You're going with us?" Jack asked her.

"Just until we catch up with the tour group. Then I'll go back. Come on, we'll wait at the door until the ranger arrives to let us in."

CHAPTER FOUR

"And if you look closely at the door you'll see bullet holes," Consuela was telling them, pointing to the top of the rounded wooden door that separated the lunchroom from the entrance to Left Hand Tunnel. "I bet you didn't know that Carlsbad was the setting for a siege that happened many years ago."

"Bullet holes?" Ashley breathed. "Are you serious?"

They all looked at the gouge marks, small and round and darkened with grime. When Sam hung back, Consuela told him, "Four young men who were, how do I put this— under the influence—stormed the lunchroom here to make a political statement about the plight of Native Americans. They demanded a million dollars and a flight to Brazil." She shook her head and said, "No one was hurt, thank heavens, but it just goes to show that people say and do the stupidest things."

That was true. People got all kinds of crazy ideas in their heads. Jack suddenly wondered if Consuela knew what Sam had said about her, but when he looked at Consuela's warm, unflinching gaze, he realized she didn't have a clue that Sam had accused her of being a drug addict. A drug addict with a needle jammed into her arm— how insane was that? People like Consuela didn't get high! The whole idea would have made him angry if he hadn't remembered that in Sam's life, all kinds of unimaginable things had happened to him every day. Ms. Lopez told them that Sam had been left to get his own food and take care of himself since he was small, and that he'd spent most of his time staring at a television set, hungry and dirty and alone. No wonder the kid was so afraid. No wonder he acted so much younger than he was. If Jack had been raised the same way, how might he have turned out? Sighing, he rubbed the top of Sam's round head. Later, when they were done with the tour of Left Hand Tunnel, he'd have to think of a way to make Sam understand that regular people were good. The people that worked for the Park Service, especially, were the best folks in the world. He'd have to straighten Sam out when they were alone, just the two of them.

"You OK, Jack?" Ashley asked, her dark eyes serious. "You're awfully quiet."

"Yeah. I'm fine. How about you, Sam? You OK?"

Sam's voice was barely above a whisper when he said, "I d-d-don't want to g-g-get shot."

"Oh, I'm sorry, maybe I shouldn't have told that story. I didn't mean for it to upset him." Crouching down, Consuela tried to take Sam's hand, but he pulled it away and clasped his hands together behind his back. If it bothered Consuela, she didn't let it show. "No one is going to hurt you, Sam. You're going to see a wonderful place, a cave full of amazing stalactites and crystals and all kinds of great things. I'll take you to the tour guide, and he'll tell you some first-rate stories. Would you like that?"

"I w-want," Sam said, struggling to get his mouth around the words.

"What do you want, sweetheart?"

"I w-w-want you t-t-to," he swallowed, twisting his lips into a tiny knot, "l-l-leave me alone."

It took a moment for the words to register on Consuela's face. Her smile froze at the corners of her mouth.

"Sam!" Ashley exploded. "That's not nice—that's rude!"

"No, it's all right. Don't bother him," Consuela said, straightening. She brushed gray dust off one knee and then the other, trying, it seemed to Jack, to keep her face even. "Well, I think I see the ranger coming who's going to unlock the door for us. You kids wait here. I'll be right back."

As Consuela walked away, Ashley turned on Sam, her braids whirring around like blades. "Sam! What are you doing? You can't talk to Consuela that way! And don't try to hide behind Jack—he's not going to protect you! I can't believe you said that!"

Sam's large eyes got even bigger as he grabbed Jack's hand. "She t-t-took d-d-drugs. W-w-with a n-n-needle—"

"Stop it, Sam. She did not! And you'd better be nice to her from now on, and maybe she'll forget the rotten thing you just did." Wagging her finger just inches from his face, Ashley snapped, "You better start smiling, Sammy, or—" the words died in her throat as Consuela came toward them with the ranger.

A very tall man wearing his Smoky Bear hat, he offered Consuela a book of matches for the lanterns. Smoke curled around her face as she lit the candles, and when she blew the match out, Jack noticed her nails had been enameled with silver nail polish. The ranger unlocked the door with a key and swung it open. "The group is only about ten minutes in front of you now—you should have no trouble catching up. How old is that little boy?" he asked, eyeing Sam.

Sam held up both hands with four fingers extended on each.

"OK," the ranger said. "Just checking. Six is the youngest age permitted on this tour, and 16 is the youngest without an adult. You're planning on staying with them, aren't you, Consuela? Policy says minors must have an adult escort."

Hesitating, Consuela admitted, "Dr. Rhodes thought that maybe just this once…actually, she was hoping the tour guide ranger would be willing to take responsibility for them. They're really good kids."

"Sorry, Consuela," the man said. "No exceptions to the rules."

Is that it? Jack wondered. Are we being turned away? Now what? Dad's gone, Mom's in a meeting—does that mean we go back up the elevator and hang around the visitor center on our own?

Biting her lip, Consuela looked at her watch, then said, not sounding too happy about it, "Well, I guess I'll just stay with them for the whole tour. Will you call upstairs to Dr. Rhodes's office and tell her I won't be back for a while?"

"Sure, I'll do that," the man told her. Then, to Jack, Sam, and Ashley, he said, "You kids ought to say a big 'thank you' to Consuela here. There's no way I could let you go without her."

"Thank you," Jack and Ashley chimed. Sam stayed silent, drilling his toe into the soft layer of dirt. Ashley shot Jack a look, but he could only shrug in reply. What was he supposed to do? Yell at Sam in front of Consuela? Ashley would just have to trust that he'd deal with it later.

With Consuela in the lead, the four of them walked through the opened door. "Enjoy," the ranger called out just as the door closed behind them with a loud groan.

Jack was unprepared for the weight of the darkness in the tunnel. Two skimpy candle flames seemed totally insufficient in that realm of shadow and bizarre shapes. "Be careful to stay on the marked path," Consuela was telling them. "These formations are delicate. You don't want to bump up against them or they might break off." Pointing, she said, "The bubbly-looking stuff on the ceiling is called popcorn. The part that makes it sparkle is called aragonite. Isn't it beautiful? And of course, the formations hanging from the ceiling are stalactites. The ones growing from the ground up are called..." she suddenly stopped talking, staring at them blankly. Tapping a finger to her forehead, she said, "Wait a minute. What are they called? I can't remember. Stalac-aragonite—no, that's not right. But it rhymes." She began whispering to herself, as if she were deep in conversation within her own mind.

"Are you talking about stalagmites?" Ashley offered.

"Yes!" Consuela smacked her palm into her forehead. "I can't believe I didn't remember. I must be losing it. But aren't they gorgeous?"

Jack didn't think they were gorgeous—to him they were almost grotesque, like sculptures from a disturbing dream. Maybe he was a little more spooked than he should have been, after all the strange things he'd heard in the past half hour, but shapes and shadows seemed to dance in the half-light, alive and possibly malevolent. Worse, he knew there were bats in the cave, even though Dr. Rhodes had said there were only a few hundred of a certain species in this particular tunnel. They were clinging unseen to the cave ceiling above his head. No! He wouldn't let his mind go on that track. Bats were friendly, safe animals. He needed to get a grip. Anyway, Consuela was in charge, and she wouldn't let anything bad happen.

They walked on, kicking up a tiny cloud of dust from

the silt that seemed to coat the trail. Gargoyle-shaped formations surrounded them on all sides; the walls themselves seemed to have been squirted with frosting from an insane baker. A bridge that spanned a chasm 40 feet deep loomed into view, which made Sam cling to him all the tighter. Consuela was still chattering, but it seemed as if she were speaking only to herself.

"OK, you don't want to fall, so you stick close to me, and I stick close to you, and we'll all be...real sticky together." Consuela giggled at that, and clutched Jack's arm.

In the eerie light from the lantern, her face appeared a little giddy! Jack couldn't really see her eyes, which were in shadow, but her smile seemed off center, and the smile stayed pasted on to her face like a comic mask. Weird! Jack thought. It had to be the lantern light that was making everything look weird.

Ashley walked ahead of them, managing to move in the circles of pale light cast by the two lanterns. Sam shuffled behind Jack, his fingers curled around the back waistband of Jack's jeans. "Quit pulling on me so hard, or you're going to yank my pants down," Jack told him. "There's enough room on the path for you to walk beside me. Anyway, there's more light up here."

"N-no," Sam answered defiantly. "I'm st-staying back." For a kid who got so easily spooked by the least little thing, Sam sure could act stubborn at times.

The tunnel tour had been really interesting up to that

point, but it was starting to turn into an ordeal for Jack, with Consuela's sharp fingernails digging into his arm and Sam's jagged fingernails scraping the skin on his back.

"It's like we're dancing," Consuela was saying. "Step step dip, step step dip...."

What was she talking about? The path was pretty level right there, with no dips or rough spots. Even so, Consuela began to stumble.

"Are you all right?" Jack asked anxiously, struggling to hold her upright. At the same time he yelled impatiently, "Sammy, let go of my pants!" As soon as he yelled it he knew he'd made a mistake, because Sam stopped dead on the path. When Jack swung the lantern around, he saw Sam's lips tremble as the tears built up in his eyes.

"I'm sorry, Sam," Jack said quickly, but he thought, Oh, great! Here I am, stuck with a crying kid and a woman who seems a little—off-center. And Ashley's up ahead, not paying any attention to what's happening. Why do I have to deal with all this by myself?

Right then, he heard a tour guide in the distance announce, "Well, visitors, here we are at The Beach. This is where we stop to experience total darkness. In a moment we'll all extinguish our lanterns and my flashlight, and then we'll see what it's like to be completely deprived of light. Are you ready?"

"Wait," Jack called out. "We're right behind you—we're supposed to join your tour."

"Come on, we're just up ahead," the tour guide called. "Can you see our light?"

"Yes, I see it," Ashley cried. When Jack pulled Sam and Consuela around a bend in the path, in front of him he saw a large group clustered in an open space that looked like an amphitheater. At least 20 people—men, women, and several kids about their age, greeted them with surprise. Jack gave a tiny wave and tried not to look as stupid as he felt. He wished Consuela would introduce them.

"Oh, Consuela, hello," a woman said, smiling pleasantly. She was a small ranger, blond, from what Jack could tell, and as thin as a sparrow. Another ranger, a man, stood at her side, his arms crossed over his thickly muscled chest. Both rangers held flashlights instead of lanterns.

"I see you brought some special guests," the woman said. "Well, there's always room for a few more. Everyone, this is Consuela Sandoval, who works in the office with our bat specialist, Dr. Rhodes. And she's brought three young friends. Welcome to our tour, little cavers!"

Was Jack supposed to answer that? "I'm Jack, and this is my sister, Ashley, and that's Sam," he said, feeling himself color as the other tourists in the group stared at him. A girl about the same age as Ashley gave a wave.

"I'm Laura," the ranger said. "My partner"—she gestured to the male ranger—"is Chuck. And you have joined us in an area we call The Beach, since it's open and the silt floor is almost like sand. Well, Jack, Ashley, and Sam, you're just in time. As I was explaining to the others, this cave is completely devoid of light, and we're all about to experience total darkness, something we don't really get on the surface."

"How come?" Ashley asked. "I mean, my room at home can get pitch black."

Laura nodded enthusiastically. "Good question. Up above, even though you might think it's dark, in actuality there is almost always at least some source of light getting in. Starlight, moonlight, light pollution from buildings—light seeps in from everywhere. But down here, deep in this cave, there's no source of illumination whatsoever. Your pupils, if you could see them in total darkness, would be all the way open and your irises would disappear. Your eyes would look almost completely black."

"Cool," Jack breathed.

"I'm going to ask you not to move around while we try this, just to be safe. So—are you all ready?"

"We're ready," the crowd answered.

"Then on the count of three, blow out your candles. One…

"Two," the crowd cried.

"Three!"

In an instant all the lanterns were blown out, all except for Consuela's. "Consuela," Jack hissed, "blow your lantern out!"

"Yes. Of course. Sorry folks," Consuela muttered, and with a quick puff of air she blew out her lantern. Jack found himself standing in absolute blackness. Except it wasn't. Images of the cave walls and ceiling appeared in front of him, like visions from a flash that lingered long after the picture was taken. Ghosts of stalactites and stalagmites floated in front of him, almost real, but phantasmic. Was his mind playing tricks on him, or could he actually see in the dark?

"Hey, I see the walls of the cave," a man in the crowd announced. "Is that normal?"

"Absolutely," Chuck's deep voice answered. "You're seeing images your brain is painting, since your brain can't decipher total blackness. The images would go away if you stayed in the dark for a while. Try waving your hand in front of your face. See anything?"

Jack could feel a slight breeze from his hand, which was probably just inches from his nose, but his brain didn't register. All he could see were strange phantom images that floated in front of his eyes. No hand, no nothing. Feeling slightly off balance with no visual reference points, he teetered a little in his sneakers.

"J-J-Jack?" Sam whispered, clutching Jack's arm in a vise-like grip. "I'm scared!"

"I'm right here, Mini-Me," Jack answered softly.

When Laura turned on her flashlight, it was surprising how much illumination one small light cast. "Now," she said, "we'll light all the lanterns again." Both rangers flicked on Bic lighters, then went from one tourist to another, holding flame to candle until all the lanterns had been lit. It felt like a solemn religious ceremony, ending with illumination that now appeared startlingly bright.

When it was over, Laura asked, "Before we resume the tour, does anyone have any questions about the part of the tunnel we've already seen?"

"Ques…," Consuela began, raising her hand. "When is the bird?"

"I'm sorry?" The ranger cupped her hand to her ear. "What was your question?" She frowned as though she weren't sure what she'd heard. "Something about a bird?"

"The bird. From the…in the car….You know. Gloves."

As Jack stared at Consuela in disbelief, her hand went slack on his arm. Almost in slow motion, she crumbled and slid to the floor of the cave with a gentle thump.

"Move back!" the tourists began shouting. "A woman's fainted here. Give her room! Give her air!"

The ranger who'd been guiding the tour knelt next to Consuela's unconscious form. "She's breathing," she murmured. The other ranger rushed to Consuela's side and put his ear to her lips. Raising her left wrist, he checked her pulse, while the rest of the group strained forward to see what had happened.

A tall young man unzipped his backpack and said, "I've got my cell phone in here—do you want me to call somebody for help? It looks like she's really out of it."

The ranger answered, "Your cell phone won't work in this tunnel. But if you'll go to the Big Room as quick as you can, there's a phone in there that connects to the visitor center up above. Tell them we have an emergency here, and we need a crew with a stretcher to be dispatched right away. And tell them they'd better call Station Four to send an ambulance."

Ashley cried softly to Jack, "What do you think is happening to her?"

"She passed out," Jack told her. "But she was talking and acting funny for at least ten minutes before we got to the tour group. Her feet were, like, all wobbly—she was hanging on to me like she couldn't stand up straight."

The ranger named Chuck had pulled off his jacket to fold it under Consuela's head. "We need a first-aid crew," he was saying. "I don't know what's wrong with her, but it's more than just a simple fainting spell."

Ashley stared wide-eyed at Jack, her lips forming words she wasn't about to speak out loud. Jack knew that both of them were thinking the same thing: Sam had seen Consuela inject herself with drugs, or so he claimed. Jack and Ashley had refused to believe him, had scolded Sam for even saying such a thing, but what if Sam had been right? "Should we tell the ranger?" Ashley whispered.

"What if something else is wrong with her?" Jack answered softly. "If we say maybe she took drugs, she could lose her job."

Consuela had begun to moan, "What am I—? Find the cat." Then, sounding angry, "Get your hands off!"

"Take it easy," Chuck told her. "You fainted."

"No I'm not. The chicken," Consuela said, slurring her

words. "Too fast."

One of the women tourists said, "She's delirious, and she's shaking. Here, put my jacket on top of her." A man leaned forward to suggest, "It could be claustrophobia. My mother-in-law had claustrophobia. When she was in small places she'd really freak out. But I don't think she ever passed out, at least I don't remember."

Chuck didn't answer because he'd lifted Consuela's right wrist and was staring at it. "Laura, shine that flashlight here," he told her. When Laura did, Chuck bent down for a closer look.

"Uh-oh," Ashley whispered. "Is he looking for needle marks?" In school, they'd been taught all about drug abuse and the signs of it.

Instead, Chuck was asking Consuela, "What's this bracelet? Can you tell me about this bracelet? This bracelet on your arm," he repeated.

Who cares about a bracelet at a time like this, Jack thought, wondering why the ranger was so insistent on examining the bracelet in the lantern light. Suddenly, Ashley said, "Hey, Jack. Turn around. Listen to me!"

"What?" Reluctantly, Jack pulled his eyes away from Consuela, who was muttering unintelligibly now.

"It's Sammy," Ashley answered. "I can't see him. Where the heck is Sammy?"

Jack looked around. "I don't know. He was right behind me a little while ago. Is he somewhere in the middle of these tourists? Is that him over there?"

"No, that's another blond kid, not Sam."

Ashley worked her way through the group, then returned to answer, "He's not here. Maybe he slipped out to the Big Room with that guy who went to make the phone call."

"He couldn't have," Jack told her. "Look, the people are so jammed up here they're blocking the path. No one can get past. And the rangers and Consuela are in front of us, so we'd have seen him if he went around them. There's no way he could have gone out of the tunnel."

Ashley bit her lip. "Then he must have gone into the tunnel," she declared. "Why would he do that?"

"Because he was mad at me."

"Mad at you? What for?"

"'Cause I sort of yelled at him a while back. But he couldn't go far into the tunnel because he can't see back there in the dark."

"Maybe he can. I think he picked up the lantern that Consuela dropped," Ashley stated. "That little brat! He's gone in there, and we'll have to go after him. Come on, Jack, before he goes too far and gets lost. Hurry!"

CHAPTER FIVE

Jack and Ashley rushed into the dark tunnel—or tried to rush. With only one lantern to light their steps, they moved cautiously, remembering what Consuela had told them about staying on the path. If they bumped into a formation, or worse, tripped and tried to catch themselves by reaching out, they could damage these amazing natural sculptures. Though it had taken the stalagmites and stalactites tens of thousands of years to form, a single misstep could destroy them.

"Sam can't have gotten very far," Ashley was saying. "It's as dark in here for him as it is for us, so he can't see any better than we can. And anyway, his legs are shorter."

"But we're not sure how much of a head start he got," Jack reminded her. "So don't blame me if—"

"Who said I was blaming you?" Ashley snapped, stopping in her tracks.

"I mean, it wasn't all my fault—you could have been keeping a watch on him, too."

"You're the one who yelled at him and made him run away," she argued. "Anyway, he's always hanging on to you.

He hardly even talks to me, so why should I take the blame if Sammy disappears in here and they have to call out a search party...." Her voice trailed off as both of them realized how bad things could actually get. "Anyway, we shouldn't panic. He can't be far."

"Maybe we should start calling him," Jack suggested.

"If we do, the rangers will hear us, and we'll get in trouble for leaving the group. I just want to get Sam and get back before anyone knows we're gone. Then none of us will be in trouble." She hesitated before asking, "Do you think Consuela's going to be OK?"

"I...I don't know. I think so. I hope so."

"Do you think she's on drugs like Sam said?"

Jack shrugged. "She was acting funny before she passed out, but I've never been around anyone who was high. It's possible she was sick with a fever or something."

"Except she didn't look sick to me. Just...weird. And all that stuff she was saying with her words backward and stuff...." Ashley sighed as Jack held up the lantern. The yellow light showed her forehead furrowed, a sure sign she was worried. "I really feel bad that I didn't believe Sam," she told Jack. "I bet that's why he ran off."

"We'll apologize when we find him. But we'd better move it or we'll never catch up to him."

They hurried on in silence, following the path as it narrowed, twisting back and forth as it pierced deep into the cave's belly. Minutes crawled by, how many Jack wasn't sure, and yet there was still no sign of Sam. They were going far—too far—although logic told Jack they had to be closing in on Sam. Jack's footsteps were muffled by the soft earth as he kicked up small clouds of cave dust that drifted and then settled back onto the sculpted stone. They rounded another bend and saw more ghostly figures, gray and lifeless, stalagmite arms outstretched as if to grab them as they walked by. Glancing behind, he could no longer make out the soft glow of the group's lanterns. There was nothing but inky blackness to his side, in front, everywhere he could see. How far had they gone? It was so hard to judge distance when there was nothing but darkness surrounding them. His heart sank as he realized they'd gone dangerously far inside the cave. What if Sam had veered off onto a side trail? What if he was hurt? How could they find someone if the person didn't want to be found? No, they would have to go back. Consuela had probably been treated and taken away by now, and the group might even be looking for them. It was time to quit trying.

Stopping next to a pillar that looked like a tall, frosted cake, he set his lantern down. "Ashley, we've gone as far as we can. We have to stop—" he began.

"No, wait! I think I've found something!" Ashley cried, grabbing the lantern. "Is that a footprint in the dirt next to the path?"

Impatient, Jack answered, "Lots of people go through this tunnel, so there are probably lots of footprints. We've got to give it up and get some help. Sam's gone."

"But this one's off the path, and it's smeared a little bit like someone might have been running, and then they sort of slipped. And look—it's going toward that narrow corridor. Do you think he would have been scared enough to go off the trail?"

"Right now, I think he could do anything." Jack knelt to get a closer look at the footprint, taking the lantern and lowering it almost to the ground. The print might have been from Sam's sneaker; it looked about the right size, with a pattern like tire treads etched in powdery silt. "If this is his, then he must have turned that way," Jack said, pointing to an even narrower corridor that forked to the left. "Sam!" he yelled. "Sammy, are you in there? Where are you? It's me and Ashley. You've got to come out, right now."

When there was no answer, Ashley shook her head. "What do you expect? If he's running away, he's not going to tell us where he is. I say we go after him."

As the older brother, Jack felt he should be the one to make the decisions, not Ashley. He was 13, Ashley only 11. So OK, decide, he told himself. Turn back, find the rangers, and ask for help? Or keep looking for Sam on their own— after all, as Ashley had said, Sam couldn't be very far ahead of them. But which direction? Should they take a chance and go into that turnoff, hoping the footprint was Sammy's and that was the way he went? Or figure it was someone else's footprint and stay on the marked path a little longer?

As Jack hesitated, Ashley cried, "Jack! Down there in that turnoff—I see a light! It's gotta be Sam's lantern. Maybe we can get him and go back before anyone knows he's been missing. Come on, let's go!" When Jack didn't move quickly enough to suit her, she said impatiently, "If you aren't coming, at least give me the lantern so I can see where I'm going."

"I'm coming, I'm coming," he grumbled. "I hope you know what you're talking about, because I don't see any light."

Ashley's braids whipped behind her as she turned toward the corridor. "Follow me!" she commanded. "You're blind as a bat."

"Bats aren't blind," he reminded her. "Dr. Rhodes said so."

The turnoff led to a much narrower tunnel, with no marked path. The more steps they took, the rougher the ground became. Then Jack saw what Ashley was talking about—a small light in the distance. Oddly, it looked green, rather than gold like the flame in Jack's lantern. Since he'd never been in a cave, he didn't know whether atmospheric differences—or whatever—might make a flame change color. The green light wasn't moving, so Sam must have stopped running. Probably he was sitting down waiting for them to find him.

Sharp, uneven rock jutted up from the narrow path, at times slowing Jack and Ashley to a snail's pace. Once, Jack missed a step and felt the bite of rock against his forearm, cold and sharp. Steadying himself, he realized with relief he hadn't broken any of the irreplaceable formations. Vowing to be even more careful, he cautiously made his way forward, one foot placed gingerly in front of the other as if he were walking a tightrope. The light ahead guided him, staring at him like a single, shimmering, green eye.

Pausing, he cupped his free hand to his mouth. "Sam," he called as loudly as he could, "we're here! You don't have to be afraid anymore."

Silence. After a moment, Jack thought he heard a single drip hit water, although he couldn't see anything but the eerie formations.

"Come on, Sammy, say something!" Ashley demanded. "Are you afraid about Consuela? She's going to be fine. Pick up your lantern and walk toward us." Another pause. "Just do it, Sammy—we've got to get back!"

Jack had always imagined that a cave would echo, but Ashley's words seemed to get sucked into the blackness. The light ahead didn't move the slightest bit.

"I guess he's going to make us go all the way up there to get him," Ashley sighed. "What a pain he's turned out to be."

It took another five minutes before Jack realized what they'd been walking toward. At first, his eyes couldn't process the fact that the light wasn't on the ground, but suspended almost four feet in the air, a small, round circle that didn't flicker or move like his own candle did. Then, when he finally got within ten feet, he understood. The light they'd been chasing hadn't been a lantern at all but rather a flat glass reflector fastened on top of a metal pole. The green glow was nothing more than a reflection of their own lantern light, a fool's gold that had drawn them far into the corridor. They'd been wasting their time; worst of all, Sam was nowhere to be found.

"Great, just great," Jack muttered. "We've been chasing air."

Ashley seemed bewildered as she stared at the reflector. "Sorry. I really thought it was Sam. What is this thing?"

"I guess it's a marker of some kind. I don't know what it's for, but it sure has messed us up. We've been gone 15, maybe 20 minutes already. You realize that the rangers are probably already looking for us. This whole thing is getting to be big trouble."

"I said I was sorry! What else do you want me to do?"

"So you agree that we've got to go back and get help now?"

Scowling, Ashley gave a terse nod. It wasn't really her fault, Jack knew. He'd gone along with her plan. But he could feel panic starting to spread through his insides, the same as when he gulped a glass of cold water on a hot day. Time was ticking by, and with each second Sammy could be getting more lost while he and Ashley could be getting into more and more trouble. What were the first instructions drilled into him every time he went camping? Stay with the group. Don't leave the trail. But here he was, wandering in a cave, away from any adult or ranger. Well, he'd be the leader now. It was time to give it up and get help.

Holding his lantern high, Jack began retracing his steps. The layer of cave dust was lighter here, which made the popcorn formations appear whiter, like real popped kernels glittering with crystals. He shuddered when he saw a half-mummified body of a bat next to the trail, and wondered how many of the creatures were in these small side passages. They don't swarm until night, he reminded himself. Just keep going. Don't think about them. Think about Sam. It was possible Sam had already returned to the tour group, and everyone was sitting at the part of Left Hand Tunnel known as The Beach, just waiting for them to show up. And Consuela—what about her? Had the medics taken her away by now? Had—

"Jack, you're going the wrong way. That's not the way we came."

"What?" Jack stopped and held the lantern to Ashley's face. Her arms were crossed tightly over her chest as if she were cold, and she was shaking her head.

"See how this tunnel splits? You're going to the left. We came from the right."

Peering into the darkness, Jack realized the trail divided like an artery. How had he missed it? But his sister was wrong—this was the path they'd walked. He was almost sure of it.

"Ashley, this is the right one. Look, when I turn around, I can see the reflector perfectly."

"But watch me. I'm walking down this path." She disappeared into the second trail. "And when I turn around," she said, her voice distant and muffled, "I can still see the reflector, too."

Jack blinked. Mentally, he tried to retrace the trail, but all of the formations had begun to look the same. Melted columns and stalactites marched alongside the trail, row after row of lifeless gray rock. Wasn't that large pear-shaped formation the exact one he'd seen earlier? Yes, now he was sure of it—he remembered thinking how round the bottom of the stone had swelled. He'd seen that formation before, which meant he was going the right way, and this time, he would listen to his own gut. Ashley would have to follow him, for once.

When his sister reappeared, he tried to sound more confident than he felt. "Ashley, I remember this trail. If we think it's wrong, we can turn back and go your way. OK?"

She hesitated, until Jack reminded her that he was the one with the light. Then, lantern high, he turned resolutely down the path he'd decided on.

As they walked, Jack wavered between absolute certainty and absolute doubt. A stalagmite that stretched up like a witch's finger was one he'd seen before; yes, he convinced himself, he was going the right way. But then he saw a group of rocks that looked like turtles crawling one over the other, and he wondered if Ashley had been right, after all, because he sure didn't remember anything that looked like that. Twice more there were splits in the path, and each time Jack tried to stay on the main trail, studying the ground for footprints that weren't there. He could make out smudges, but were they from their feet or from others who'd been there long ago? In this windless tunnel, footsteps could last for years, couldn't they? Ashley had grown quiet, which made Jack even more nervous. He almost wished she'd insist that they go back. One thing was sure, they should be hitting the main trail any minute. Any minute now…any….

He tried to mark their progress by the time that had passed, but because he hadn't checked his watch when they'd started, he wasn't sure how long it had been. His instincts told him the trail should be right up ahead. The passageway narrowed so that he had to turn sideways, his right arm outstretched. No, he hadn't had to do that before. This was all wrong! Good grief! Where were they?

Ashley, for once, didn't say "I told you so." Instead, she flattened herself as much as she could against the rock and motioned for Jack to step around her and go first.

"We haven't lost that much time," she told him. "We'll get back to that one fork, and then we'll get back to the main trail. It's no big deal."

Sometimes it seemed as if his sister could read his thoughts. He just nodded and moved to the front, the lantern swaying in his hand.

The first thing he realized was that he could no longer see the reflector. It had disappeared from view, which meant that they'd definitely gone the wrong way. Jack rubbed the back of his neck with his left hand and tried not to panic. They'd stay on the trail and retrace their steps. Simple.

Another five minutes crawled by, and they came to another split in the trail, or maybe it was the same one. How many times might they have doubled back to the same fork in the dark without even recognizing it? Bewildered, Jack had no clue which way to go. He hoped Ashley would.

Apparently she didn't. "Oh-h man," Ashley wailed. "Do you know which direction we should take?"

Jack put his arm around his sister's thin shoulders in reply. "It's not time to panic yet," he told her.

"Why not?" Her voice was shrill.

"Because there can't be that many trails back here. Because even if we do get lost, the rangers will come looking. We'll be fine—"

When Jack heard the sound, the words he'd been speaking died in his throat. Somewhere in the blackness swelled a strange, eerie noise, guttural and low. Ashley stared at him, wide-eyed, her lips parted.

"Jack—"

"Shush," he whispered. "There it is again."

It was hard to tell how close the sound might be, but Jack guessed it couldn't be too much more than 50 feet away. It wailed, high, then low, like a cat in the dead of night. Images of Goatsuckers crowded into his head. A shadow to his left seemed to move on its own—Jack's insides turned to ice.

He could feel his sister's arm encircle him, her fingers tightening around his waist. Then another cry rose up like a specter's shriek.

It was definitely time to panic.

CHAPTER SIX

Jack and Ashley clung to one another in terror, as
the lantern light cast their own shadows into huge
shapes on the cave walls. For what seemed like
an hour but was probably little more than minutes,
the terrifying sound wafted through the darkness,
now loud, now soft. Jack's first impulse was to run away
from it, as fast as he could, as far as he could. Then,
slowly, fear began to loosen its hold on his brain, enough
that he recognized that the cries were coming from a
human. From a very young human.

Sam!

The cries were so eerie!—nothing like the wails an
ordinary child would make. They sounded strangled,
alternating between low guttural rasps and then high,
muted shrieks. It was as if Sam had never learned to just
let loose and cry out his pain, as if he'd always had to
hide his fear—or else be punished for showing it. What
kind of hurts did he have from his past life? Jack had
never heard a sound like that coming from any human
being. The sound made his skin crawl.

"It's Sam!" Jack told Ashley. "Don't call out to him or he might stop. We need to follow his crying so we know where to go."

"Are you sure it's him?"

"Who else would it be?" he asked, impatient.

Ashley didn't answer, but Jack knew what she was thinking. Trolls. Blood-sucking bats. Cave ghosts haunting the bizarre formations. But this sound was all too human, and they couldn't let their imaginations take them off into the netherworld. The two of them had to get a grip on reality.

All around them they heard the drip of water falling from the cave ceiling into small puddles, mostly invisible except when the lantern light skimmed the surface with golden brushstrokes. His own shallow breathing and the shuffle of his shoes filled his ears, but above it all, he heard those heart-wrenching sobs of a little lost boy. Once, Jack picked a finger tunnel that dead-ended, and another time Ashley made a wrong turn that took them away from the eerie wailing. At last they reached him, alone, sitting in complete darkness, his arms around his legs and his round head bowed. The knees of his jeans were covered with a soft layer of cave dust. His hands looked grimy, even in the half-light.

"Sammy, we're here," Jack called softly. "It's me, Jack."

"And me, too. Ashley."

Sam raised his head to stare at them with the most desolate expression Jack had ever seen. "I a-b-b-bout d-d-died," he sobbed. Pressing the tips of his fingers into his eyes, he dropped his chin onto his chest and let out another sob.

"No you didn't about die; you just got lost." Jack knelt beside Sam and awkwardly patted his back, his hand making *rat-ta-tat-tat* sounds on the fake-leather jacket that covered Sam's thin shoulder blades. "No worries. We're going to take you back. The tour rangers are probably already looking for us by now. That's bad, because we'll get in big trouble for leaving the trail—but good, because we'll just follow them out of here." The words sounded far more confident than Jack really felt. "Hey, where's your lantern?"

"There," Sammy answered, pointing to a spot a few feet away.

Picking up their own lantern and holding it above her head, Ashley peered into the darkness. "Where?'" she asked. "I don't see it."

"In the h-h-hole."

"What hole?" She took a few steps down the trail, swinging the light from side to side. "Oh my gosh! Look!" she shrieked. "Jack, come here!" In an instant Jack was on his feet and next to his sister. Close enough behind her that one misstep could have spelled tragedy, Jack saw a drop-off, a black pit that yawned so deeply there was no way to see the bottom.

"In there?" he asked Sam. "You dropped your lantern down there?"

"I didn't m-m-mean to. I f-f-fell."

Jack pictured it in his mind: Sam running away across this rough cave floor, barely able to see in the wavering light of a single candle, then tripping. The lantern would have flown out of his hand into that chasm that seemed to have no end. What if not only the lantern but also Sammy had fallen into that pit! Maybe he really would have died. Jack shuddered, and not just from the 56-degree coolness of the cave.

"It's all right, Sam," Ashley told him, her voice soothing him the way Olivia would have done. "You're OK. That's what's important. Stand up and hold my hand. It's time to get out of here."

"J-J-Jack's hand," Sam insisted.

"Fine," she sighed. "Jack's hand. This time, I'll lead the way. I think I can remember which way we came. We should have been dropping breadcrumbs or something so we could find our way out."

"I th-th-thought you c-c-couldn't leave things in a c-c-cave."

"I know. I was joking, Sam, about something in the tale of Hansel and Gretel. But even without crumbs I can do this. I think I know exactly where we are." She smiled a half-smile, but Jack wasn't fooled at all. How could she know anything after all the wrong turns they'd made? Were other chasms waiting to catch them, to trap them as they stumbled through the darkness? How lost could they get in this maze of tunnels? The truth was, neither one of them knew which path would lead them out, and that meant they could be walking deeper into the bowels of the cave instead of toward the main path. He could already feel his stomach rumble, a reminder that he should have eaten more for lunch, especially since there was nothing back here to chew on but dust. Dust and the few cave crickets he might be lucky enough to catch. Don't be stupid, he chided himself. They'd be out of Left Hand Tunnel and into the cafeteria in a matter of minutes. An hour, tops. Let Ashley lead the way. She couldn't do any worse than he had.

They trudged silently, Ashley's lantern bobbing with each step and Sam's sweaty hand firmly grasping Jack's. Sam was one step behind, following Jack as though he were a dog and Jack's arm the leash. The hand-holding made Jack feel slightly off balance, so after a while he tried to pry Sam free, but Sam clung even tighter until his nails bit into Jack's skin like tiny teeth.

"Hey, not so tight, Bud," Jack told him. "Wait a second, Ashley."

His sister stopped and turned.

"You can walk alone, can't you?" Jack asked Sam.

Sam shook his head. "I d-d-don't want to f-f-f-" He took a breath, and tried again, his face twisting as he struggled to get out the word. "F-f-f-f-"

"Fall?"

Sam nodded.

"Follow right where I walk, and you'll be fine. Just don't run. That's how you lost your lantern."

"Why did you take off and run like that in the first place, Sam?" Ashley asked. "Is it because we didn't believe you about Consuela?"

Shrugging, Sam looked at the floor. He scuffed his sneaker into the soft earth until he made a small, moon-like crater.

"Because listen, whatever is wrong with Consuela, I don't think it's drugs."

More silence. Jack heard Ashley's soft breathing and heard another drip hit an invisible puddle. Sam stubbornly pressed his lips together, refusing to answer even when Ashley continued to press him. It was pointless, Jack decided. Whatever Sam had seen, they'd have to unravel it later. Right now, they needed to find the main trail and get back to the surface. He wanted to feel the burning sun on his face and breathe the clean desert air. The cool, damp air of the cave was beginning to feel suffocating.

"Come on, we'll talk about all that when we're out of here. It's been an hour since we left the trail. We need to get back before people start to freak." Ten minutes farther, they hit a fork in the trail. "Which way, Ashley?"

Ashley pointed with her free hand. "That way, I think."

They turned a corner where the pale rock looked porous, with shallow cavities that pocked the cave walls like bone, and for a moment Jack felt as though he were inside a skull. He didn't remember seeing this part of the cave before. How far back did the other passages go? Mentally he tried to picture the map he'd seen of Left Hand Tunnel, which was filled with small offshoots that looked like roots on a tree. One offshoot connected to another. It might be possible, he realized, to wander in this labyrinth for days! He was just about to say something when Ashley touched his back and told him, "Up ahead! It's the green reflector. See, I told you we were going the right way. You know, I really was getting a little bit worried, but now that I see the reflector I think we're going to be all right. I know exactly where we are!"

But when they reached the metal stake, Jack quickly realized that they were back at the forks in the path, either of which could be the right one. Or both could be wrong. Now what? Ashley stood, her mouth slightly agape. Arm extended, she held the lantern to each opening, the light bouncing off the strange formations until it disappeared into the blackness beyond. Nothing ahead of them seemed right. She looked to Jack, her eyes asking for help, but Jack could only shake his head in reply. With a sinking feeling, he faced the truth he hadn't wanted to let himself comprehend. They were lost.

"J-J-Jack," Sam asked softly, "are we g-g-going to d-d-die?"

"No, we are not going to die. Don't panic. The first thing we need to do is to get some kind of plan." He rubbed his forehead, as if the friction might get some ideas sparking inside his brain. "Ashley, put the lantern in the center so I can see. Sam, let go of my hand and sit down. I've got to think."

The three of them dropped to the coolness of the floor. Rough stone pushed into his back as Jack leaned against the cave wall. Ashley and Sam pulled their legs beneath them and looked to him expectantly, as though any moment now he'd have the answer. Except he didn't have a clue what to do next. They were lost in a cave with no food, no water, no map, and only one half-melted candle for light among the three of them. By now, park rangers must have mounted a search party, fanning out a team into the cave to find them and bring them home. But where were their rescuers? Since Jack had first checked his watch, another hour had passed, plenty of time to pull a team together to search for three lost kids. One thought nagged him, though: If the rangers were looking for them, why couldn't Jack hear anything except an occasional drip of water? The cave itself seemed silent as a tomb.

What had he learned in scouting? When you're lost, you stay put and wait for help to come to you. But that was when you're lost in the wilderness, right? Did they ever say anything about caves? It didn't matter—the principle was the same. If the three of them kept going farther, that might only make it worse.

"I have an idea," Ashley announced. "The trail splits into three and there are three of us. I think each one of us should take a trail, since one of them has to be right. Whoever gets out to the main trail first could find the rangers and tell them where we are, and then—"

"No!" Jack said emphatically. "We're not splitting up." He watched Ashley stiffen. "Just listen to me!"

"No!"

"Why not?"

"I th-th-think we should do what J-J-Jack s-says," Sam broke in.

"Oh, big surprise there," Ashley snapped. "You always do everything he says. What is it, a guy thing? Why can't you ever listen to me?"

Sam looked at her, wide eyed.

"Since you believe everything Jack says, maybe you should have asked him about running off the way you did. He would have told you not to do it. Then maybe we wouldn't be in this mess."

"Hey, don't be going after Sam," Jack warned her. "That's not going to help anything. Besides, Ashley, you're the one who said you knew which trail to take. You've made mistakes, too. You're the one who was so sure that you knew the way out—"

"So now it's my fault?" Ashley exclaimed, her eyes blazing in the half-light. "You're blaming me? You're the one who wanted to find Sam without the rangers' knowing—"

"That's because I didn't want him—any of us—to get in trouble."

"Well, we're all in trouble now."

"Quit being such a drama queen. OK, so maybe we're lost now, but the rangers are going to find us. We'll get in trouble for making them put together a search, but we'll be all right."

"What if they're not looking?"

The question caught Jack by surprise. It took a moment for the idea to register.

"What if no one has figured out that we're gone?" Ashley said, snapping her braids behind her back. "Have you even thought of that? I have. Consuela's the only one in Left Hand Tunnel who knew for sure we were taking the cave tour, and she passed out. Maybe she's still unconscious. An unconscious person can't talk. An unconscious person can't ask about us, or tell about us, or anything!"

Jack began to feel sick. "So what's your point?"

"My point is we can't wait. We each need to take a trail and try to find the main path and get help. We've got to get out of here!"

Sam put his hands over his ears. Shutting his eyes, he began to rock back and forth.

"Stop it, Ashley. You're scaring Sam!"

"I'm scared."

Jack could tell she was. Sometimes, when she was truly frightened, his sister would grab her sides and hold herself tight, as if she could almost turn herself inside out. She was doing that now, clutching her sides so that Jack could see the jut of her knuckles gleaming white in the candlelight. The worst thing any of them could do now was to lose control. The second worst thing would be to turn on each other.

"Look, I know you think we should each take a tunnel, but it won't work. We can't split up."

"Why?"

"Because we only have one lantern. You can't walk without light. Someone could fall into one of those holes. We can't risk it."

Ashley was silent for a moment. She seemed to sag a little, her head falling forward as if it were suddenly too heavy for her neck. "Then what do you think we should do?" Her words were directed at the cave floor.

"We need to stop moving and wait for them to come to us. They'll find us, Ashley. I promise they will."

CHAPTER SEVEN

"Hello! We're here! Help!"

Jack and Ashley took turns calling out, but their words seemed to get sucked away into nothingness, and after a while they decided to pace themselves and shout at intervals of ten minutes, no oftener than that, to keep their throats from getting raw. Minutes dragged as they waited. It felt to Jack as though they were marking time under dark, murky water. He shifted whenever his legs got numb from sitting. Even in the half-light he could tell his hands and his clothes had become encrusted with gray dust. He sighed and looked for the hundredth time at his watch, which cast an eerie green glow against his skin. 5:32. By now, his parents must have been told that the three of them were lost. In his mind he could picture their panicked reaction; his dad would insist every single ranger be sent to comb the cave, and his mother would probably call in the SWAT team. The fact that his folks would know exactly what to do to get them out of Left Hand Tunnel reassured him. Any minute now, they'd be found. Any minute. Patience was the key.

"Hello! Help—we're back here!"

Shifting again, Jack wrapped his fingers around the lantern, feeling its warmth but blocking some of the light. From the shadows, he heard his sister speak. "You cold?"

"Maybe a little, but not as much as I figured I'd be. I thought caves were supposed to stay around 56 degrees, but this feels warmer than that. How 'bout you? Do you feel cold?"

"I was warmer when we were moving."

"Then get up and walk around."

"Maybe I will." But Ashley stayed put, sprawled on her side. With her cheek propped in her palm, she looked more like she was sunning on a beach instead of waiting in a cave. Her voice flinty, she asked, "How long now?"

"Two hours. Well, two hours and seven minutes and thirty-three seconds since we sat down, not that I'm counting or anything. The way I figure it, we got off the trail to look for Sam around 2:30. After we found him we walked around for about an hour, and then we've been sitting here for just over two. Not that long to get a rescue team together to find us."

"Soooo—three hours plus some minutes," Ashley said. "Where the heck are the rangers?"

Jack could hear the testiness in his own tone as he answered, "They're out there."

"If they are, they're sure being quiet. Listen—I don't hear

a thing. You'd think rescuers would make a little noise."
When she stopped speaking, silence enveloped them once
again. Jack heard a single drop of water hit a pool somewhere in the distance, an empty, hollow note, and then it
was still as a tomb.

"I already told you, sound might not travel too well
in caves," he told Ashley.

"Then why are we calling out if the sound won't go?"

"Because it's better than doing nothing!" he snapped.
At the tone of Jack's voice, Sam raised his head, then
dropped it back onto his arms. Taking a breath, Jack said,
"Look, Ashley, the Park people, they've got to know we're
down here. They'll find us. The rangers are probably making up a map—you know, figuring out their plan of attack.
Bet they're going in a certain order, tunnel by tunnel, one at
a time. That way they won't mess up."

"But what if—"

"Hey, you OK, Sam?" Jack interrupted, deliberately
changing the subject. "You haven't been talking much.
Not at all, really. You all right?"

"I have to g-go to the b-b-bathroom."

Uh-oh. Now what? Jack wondered. "Can't you wait?"

"How long is he supposed to wait?" Ashley asked irritably.
"Another three hours? Just take him somewhere, quick."

"Where? You're talking like there's a rest room right
around the corner."

"I don't know where, and I don't want to know," she

answered. "It's a guy thing. Just find someplace where I can't see you or hear you and get it over with."

That wasn't hard. All they had to do was walk 20 feet from where Ashley sat and she wouldn't be able to see them, as long as Jack shielded the lantern with his hand. As for hearing them—he wasn't going to worry about that.

When he and Sam returned from their little side trip, Sam slumped back onto the ground, lowered his head, and once again stopped talking. Silent as the stone, he faced the wall, biting the edge of his thumbnail. When Ashley told him to stop, he quickly switched to biting his bottom lip instead, which Ashley chose to ignore.

"Hello—we're back here."

Jack's cry hung in the air, like words in a cartoon bubble. A thick, black silence settled over them, dark and heavy. No one seemed to want to say much. After half an hour Jack told them they should get a drink, since it was important to stay hydrated. Following the sound of the drips, he led them to a cave puddle a hundred feet from where there were sitting, a clear pool invisible except for the candle's golden reflection. Ashley was the first to try, squatting down on all fours and lapping the water like a dog. Raising her head, she said it tasted fine, and Sam drank it without comment. When the cool water slipped down his own throat, Jack realized how thirsty he'd become. From years of scouting he knew that the problem in staying healthy when lost wasn't lack of food, but liquid.

It took a month to starve but only hours to dehydrate. Shaking his head, he drove the thought from his mind. They'd only be here a little longer, at the most. Any minute now they'd be found.

"Hello. We're back here. Anybody?"

Silence. The cave was silent as a—tomb! That phrase kept coming back to haunt Jack's brain, like a gong that wouldn't stop ringing. He needed to get some real conversation going here, especially with Sam, who seemed to be shrinking deeper and deeper inside himself.

"Come on, Sammy, talk to me," he urged. Sam didn't respond when Jack prodded him with questions, when he brought up stupid things Ashley had done at school, or talked about their visits to other parks. Nothing worked. Sam stared off in the darkness, his eyes vacant, his shoulders hunched, hands limp, and after a while, Jack gave up. Sam would be OK once they were out of Left Hand Tunnel, which would be any minute now. Things always seemed worse when wrapped in darkness.

"Hello—we're back here. Help us."

6:41. Leaning against the wall, Jack let his mind wander. Formations that looked like giant mushrooms seemed to sprout from the walls, and his thoughts began to connect in patterns as crazy as the cave ornaments. In his mind's eye he could almost see the Elk Refuge, 50 acres of flat marsh bristling with cattail and wild geese where his mother worked with wild animals. The Refuge was ringed by low mountains, not the majestic Tetons but smaller, plainer hills that seemed to hold the marshes in the palms of their hands. A few shallow caves had been carved by the howling Jackson Hole wind, nothing like the deep, twisting caverns of Carlsbad, but little caves that seemed to pockmark the yellow stone. A family of cougars was said to live in one of them, and the smaller ones were supposedly filled with snakes, although Jack didn't believe either story. He remembered pointing out the caves to Sam, telling him he'd take him on a hike someday, but Sam had resolutely shaken his head no. Later, the social worker, Ms. Lopez, explained that Sam had hardly ever been out of his cramped apartment, that he'd been left in front of the television set for hours and hours, which was one of the reasons he was so fearful of new things. Now, as Jack looked at Sam's round head, he wondered how much more skittish Sam would be after all this time lost in the underbelly of Carlsbad. Sam seemed to be getting lost, too, but in a different way. He was disappearing inside himself.

Where were the rangers?

By the time Jack's watch beeped 7:00, he knew something was definitely wrong. Ashley knew it, too. She kept looking at him from beneath lowered lashes, as a kind of wordless shorthand passed between them.

Where are they? Ashley seemed to ask, to which Jack replied, How should I know?

Do you want to try to leave? to which Jack answered,

No, not yet. Stay put. Don't panic.

Neither one of them wanted to upset Sam by saying it out loud, but they had to face the possibility that they might not be found before nightfall, which was a strange thought since night was endless here. The cold fact remained that they'd been gone close to four and one-half hours, and no one had found them. How was that even possible? Jack raged inside his head. Left Hand Tunnel wasn't that big, was it? Jack couldn't understand it, but his not comprehending didn't change a thing. They were lost, and they were alone. This could get serious.

As his empty stomach gave a rumble, Jack realized he was hungry. "Clean out your pockets to see if there's anything in them we can eat," he told Ashley and Sam.

None of them found much. In addition to a dried-out granola bar shoved in a corner of his jacket pocket, Jack found an old cherry cough drop and 11 cents, while Ashley produced a pack of gum, warmed from her sitting on it, which they agreed to leave unchewed for a while, just in case. Sam, though, gave them the best find—a book of matches from the Carlsbad airport.

"Matches—that's great!" Jack enthused. "We could really use them. Man, I can't believe we lucked out this way! Not that we're going to be here very long, but…."

"My m-m-mom c-c-collects matchbook c-covers," Sam answered softly. "It's for h-h-her."

Since those were the first words Sam had actually

spoken in ages, Jack nodded at him encouragingly, but Sam seemed to dry up. His fist closed around the matchbook, tight.

"I need the matches, Sam." When Sam hesitated, Jack added, "Please. We'll get you some more when we leave Carlsbad. OK?"

Sam slowly loosened his grip. Without waiting for a reply, Jack snatched the matches and pocketed them. Those were more precious than the food.

"Are you going to build a fire?" Ashley asked.

"We could, except we don't have anything to burn."

"How about some of our clothes?"

"You volunteering yours?"

Ashley clutched her sweatshirt tightly under her chin. "No."

"I'm just joking—none of us have clothes that'd make a decent fire. Everything's at least half polyester, which means they'd just smoke, and then we'd end up choking to death. Besides, we'd get way more warmth from wearing our clothes than from any fire we could make. We—we might be here a while. Not too much longer, but…" Jack hesitated. Resting his head against the rock, he focused once again on the problem staring him right in the face, a problem bigger than food and almost as big as water. Light. Illumination. The six inches of white wax had melted to four, then three, and now it was hovering dangerously close to two. Two inches, and then what? He'd sounded so sure when he'd announced that they'd be rescued if they stayed in one spot, but would they be? If the candle burned to nothing, they'd have no illumination; that slender piece of wax had become their lifeline. He shuddered, picturing the inky blackness that would envelope them when the last of the candle melted away, but he didn't want to let on how bad it could be, especially with Sam acting as spooked as he was. With the matches, Jack had another option. He just prayed they'd be rescued before he'd have to do it, but....

"Hello—Earth to Jack," Ashley said, waving her hands in the air. "What are you going to do with the matches? Heat the granola bar?"

"The candle's burning low," he answered slowly. He might as well say it—there was no way around the problem. He tried to keep his voice emotionless as he stated, "I'd say we have two more hours of light—tops."

Ashley's eyes widened. It was obvious she hadn't thought of that.

"Not that it's a problem right now," he rushed on when he saw panic ignite in Sam's face, "but unless the rangers show up soon, we'll have to blow out the candle and then relight it later, you know, to sort of pace it. That's why it's so great that we can relight—"

"No!" Sam cried. It was as if he'd suddenly come to life. Rocking forward onto his knees, his face contorted as he choked, "I h-h-hate th-th-the d-d-dark. B-b-bad things h-h-hap-p-pen in the d-d-dark. N-n-no, no, n-no!"

"OK, OK, we won't blow it out, Sammy, at least not yet." Ashley was instantly at Sam's side, her arms encircling his shoulders, and for once he let her hold him. "Shhh. It'll be all right. We'll wait." Then, to Jack, "What is wrong with him? He's shaking like a rabbit."

Jack had no idea what to do. The blood had drained from Sam's face, leaving his skin deathly white in the candlelight. He looked like a ghost, like a troglodyte or a cave imp. Fear had distorted his features.

"P-p-promise m-me! L-leave the c-c-candle burning!"

"But we can't afford to waste—"

"It's all right, we'll let it burn for now," Ashley told Sam soothingly. She settled in next to Sam's small form, so close there wasn't enough space for a credit card between them. Ashley's head, thin and oval-shaped, rested against the top of Sammy's so that a braid hung right in his face until he pushed it away. Jack got closer, too, patting Sam's leg awkwardly. He wasn't as good at this as his sister was, but Sam quickly moved from Ashley to sidle up next to Jack. If that bothered Ashley, she didn't let on.

"P-p-promise. P-p-promise."

"OK. Why are you so scared of the dark, Sam?" she asked, keeping her voice smooth. "Didn't anyone ever tell you there's nothing in the dark that's not there in the light? Why not?" she asked after Sam shook his head defiantly.

Sam looked away. His face began to settle back

to normal. He hugged his knees tight, but didn't hide his eyes.

"You can tell us. Jack's your friend. I'm your friend. We're stuck here, with absolutely nothing to do until the rescuers get here. So why don't you explain—what are you so afraid of in the dark?"

Sam blinked. Ashley's quiet tone seemed to have softened him at the edges. After a few gulping breaths he said, "M-my d-d-dad—m-my d-d-dad—"

"It has something to do with your dad?" Ashley coaxed. "What?"

"He d-died." Sam swallowed again, hard, his lips twisting as he fought against himself. It seemed as though the words stuck somewhere inside him, beneath his tongue, strangled in his throat. It took him a full ten seconds to push out the words, "In the d-d-dark. W-w-with m-m-me."

Jack felt his muscles tense. Had he heard that right? Sam's father was dead? "You were there, Sam? When your dad died?"

Sam nodded silently.

"Was your mom there, too?"

Sam shook his head no.

"So you were all alone with your dad? Wow." Jack murmured. "That's rough." He wanted to ask how Sam's dad had died, but thought he'd better not. He wasn't really sure he wanted to know.

"How old were you when it happened?" Ashley

asked gently.

"F-f-five. He over-over—My dad overd-d-d-"

"Overdosed?" It was worse than Jack had expected. Poor Sam.

"And it was m-m-my f-f-fault."

Ashley stiffened indignantly. "Your fault—how could it be your fault?"

"I-I-I c-couldn't t-t-talk," another pause, and then a tortured, "r-r-right. M-m-mom t-t-told m-m-me. M-m-my f-f-fault. It w-was d-d-dark. I c-c-couldn't c-c-call 911. I-I-I tr-tried to c-c-call, but I c-couldn't t-talk r-r-right. I'm a f-f-freak!" He slammed his fist into his forehead and shouted, "A f-f-freak! A f-freak in the d-d-dark!"

"Sam—" Jack began. But Sam wouldn't stop the rush of broken, twisted words.

"I—" His face pinched before he squeezed out, "And today, Con-Con—"

"Consuela?"

Sam nodded. "I c-c-couldn't t-t-tell. I c-couldn't h-h-help."

"You thought you couldn't help?" Ashley repeated. "Sam, is that why you ran? Because that was not your fault either. I couldn't help her, and neither could Jack. Sometimes things just happen. You're not a freak!"

"I d-d-don't want the d-d-dark."

Jack felt utterly helpless. The candle would disappear, millimeter by millimeter, unless someone came for them, but that was a plan that they couldn't seem to count on.

Why hadn't anyone found them? What was he supposed to do with a hysterical kid and a candle that was about melted down?

"Help! We're back here—in the cave!" he shouted between cupped hands. Nothing. Everything he'd done had gone hopelessly wrong. First chasing Sam, then getting lost, and now waiting—what was the right thing to do?

Rolling to his feet, he took the lantern to the intersection and peered once again down the three arms of the tunnels, shaped like a Y. It felt as though he were in an absurd game show, choosing what was behind door number one, or maybe two, or three. If he chose wrong and the light burned out…but could he just sit there, waiting? Sam was losing it. And so was Jack.

That's when he heard it—the soft *whiff, whiff,* slicing through air like knife blades. In the distance he saw a flash of light, no bigger than a dime, hovering against the ceiling.

They'd been found.

CHAPTER EIGHT

"Here we are! Over here!" Jack shouted into the darkness. "Can you see us? Help! We're over here!"

He waited, but there was no answering call, just that *whiffing* that sounded almost like rainfall. And that tiny wink of light. Another reflector? No, the light was moving, fast, like a flash of moonlight on water. Then more tiny lights began to appear, all of them in motion, in a rush, in a swarm. Behind Jack—beside him—around him—ahead of him. Those tiny lights—a dozen, 20….And the sound grew louder into a…a…beat of wings!

"Bats!" Jack cried, throwing his arms around wildly to brush them away. Bats, so close he could reach out and touch them. As they buzzed past his head, he could feel waves of disturbance in the air current; it made him shudder. It was one thing to see bats streak into the night sky, but another to be within inches of them.

"Bats—with lights?" Ashley asked, incredulous. "Look at them. They're like fireflies."

In the candlelight, Jack could see more of them coming. "I don't know what the lights are from, but they're bats.

Lots of them." They swarmed above him, higher now, farther ahead of him, with their small, grotesque features hidden by the darkness, except for those tiny lights, which might have been reflections shining from their eyes. But to make a reflection, there had to be a source of light, and the only light in the cave was the wavering, sputtering flame from their lantern, hardly bright enough to reflect in a mirror.

"I d-d-don't like this," Sam stammered.

"Yeah, well I don't either," Jack agreed. "They're way too close for me. They'll be gone soon, Sam. I think they're swarming, like we saw the first night." How long ago had that been? It seemed that an age had passed since he and his parents had witnessed the bat flight in the amphitheater.

Then it clicked into his brain—the bats were flying out toward the cave entrance for their nightly emergence. They were leaving the cave. The bats knew the way to the outside.

"Quick—follow them!" he yelled.

"Go after the bats? Why?" Ashley demanded.

"They'll lead us out. Follow the bats!"

With Jack going first, holding the lantern high, they stumbled after the bats, moving as fast as they could over the uneven floor in the near darkness. But the bats knew the way, and Jack did not. The bats had an echolocation system perfected over millions of years; Jack lurched forward, unsure whether he was moving toward a tunnel or only into the shadows ahead of and to the sides of him. He could hear Ashley's rapid breathing and Sam's jagged panting as they pushed to keep up.

"Hurry!" Jack cried as the tiny flashes of light grew even smaller. "They're getting away!"

"Ouch! Jack stop!"

When he spun around, he could see Ashley's thin form sprawled on the ground. Sam, his hands clamped under her shoulder, was trying to pull her to her feet. A dark smudge of dirt cut across her left cheek; rocking onto her knees, she stood, clutching her elbow as if she had a broken wing.

"Are you OK?" Jack cried.

"I don't know—I think so." Gingerly, she felt her arm. "I didn't see the rock sticking up, and—"

"That's OK. Let me get a look at it." Setting the lantern down, Jack pushed up her sleeve and inspected her arm. As quickly and as gently as he could, he moved the joint forward and back while Sam watched, wide-eyed. Ashley winced when Jack rotated the elbow to the left. Between gritted teeth she said, "I'm all right."

"I don't think it's broken," he told her quickly. When he looked overhead, he saw two dim lights buzz by. The rest of the tiny lights had sped forward in the darkness. The bats had almost disappeared.

"There're just a few stragglers still flying," he told Ashley. "If we don't follow them right now, they'll all be gone."

"I know," she replied, her voice grim.

"I'll st-stay here and h-h-help Ash-sh-shley," Sam said. "Y-you g-g-go ahead, Jack."

"No," Jack told him. "We keep together."

Down a twisted tunnel and around another bend, Jack tried to keep his eyes on the ceiling while watching his step on the rough terrain. It was slower going now; Sam clutched Ashley's good arm, trying to keep her steady, while Jack fought back his own impatience. Blackness pressed in on him as he tried to follow the very few remaining chips of light that shot past him like bullets in the dark, until there were no more bits, just endless, unbroken blackness. He stopped at yet another turnoff, straining to see any flash that could tell him which way to go. Once again, the lantern light was swallowed up as he held it into the mouth of each path. Once again, he had no clue which way to go. The contest had been too uneven. The bats had won the race.

"Now what? What should we do now? Where are the bats!" Ashley cried, straining to see.

Jack blinked hard before answering. "Gone."

"Are w-we even m-m-more l-lost now?" Sam stammered. "Are we?"

"I don't know. Maybe." Jack stood there, feeling help-less. The weight of it pushed on him, as heavy as the gloom around them. He looked at the lantern, burning dangerously low, and into the frightened faces of Sam and

Ashley. Running after the bats had been his idea, and it should have been a good one because the bats were on their way out of the cavern. Or were they? He didn't know that much about bats, especially bats with little flickers of light shining from them. Did that mean they were a different species? Maybe these bats stayed inside the caverns all the time and just flew from one cave to another. So he might have been following an illusion.

Dejected, Ashley slid down onto the ground, her hurt arm held at a right angle from her body. "I thought we were really going to get out of this place. Why doesn't anyone come for us? We could die back here and no one—"

"Stop it!" Jack told her, more harshly than he meant to. "You'll get Sam all worked up, and that's the last thing we need. Give me a minute; I'll think of something." But the truth was, Jack was coming close to losing it, too. Being responsible for his younger sister and an eight-year-old boy meant he had to keep himself under control, when he really wanted to scream out his own frustration at these unforgiving cave formations, this wicked maze that had them trapped in its black maw. But he couldn't lose it, not now. Ashley and Sam were looking to him for answers. Even though he didn't have any, he couldn't afford to let himself panic.

"Now listen," he told them, keeping his voice even. "We know we were going in the right direction because we followed the bat flight to this point." Yeah, he told himself, that is, if those bats were actually on their way out. But what did he know about it? Nothing! "We just have to keep trailing them," he finished lamely.

"How can we trail them if we can't see them?" Ashley asked. "Did they go to the right or to the left? Do we take door number one or two?"

"I'm not sure. So I'm going to let you pick. Which way should we go, Ashley? You have a 50 percent chance of being right."

"I don't want to pick—"

"Th-there." Sam said, pointing down a tunnel. "It's this w-w-way."

"You sure, Sammy?" Jack asked.

Sam nodded.

Sam's guess was as good as anyone's, Jack supposed. "OK then. Door number two it is." Even as he said it, he saw that the candle had burned perilously close to the bottom of the lantern. "Let's move it!" he barked.

After that, no one spoke. They trudged along in silence, making slow progress because it was so hard to see. Although the cave was supposed to be only 56 degrees Fahrenheit, it felt warmer, and Jack began to sweat. The candle had begun to sputter, a sign that the flame would soon die. Then what would they do? He was beginning to formulate a plan where he would shred his shirt to make a wick, when suddenly, Ashley whispered, "Stop!"

"Why?" he asked.

"Shhhh. Be quiet. I hear something—I don't know what it is."

Then Jack heard it too. A scraping noise, somewhere ahead of them in the blackness. That was all. Like someone's fingernails clawing at the calcite walls of the cave.

"Is it bats?" Ashley whispered.

"Doesn't sound like any noise a bat would make." But then, Jack had no idea what sounds bats might make, and he couldn't give the matter enough attention because Sam's hand, holding tightly to his, had begun to tremble. "It's OK," he hissed to Sam. "Don't be scared."

And then, very clearly, they heard a man's deep voice saying, "Just what are these here cave balloons we're stealing?"

Another voice answered, "Don't say 'stealing.' It's such a harsh word."

"You college students!" the deeper voice scoffed. "Don't you know it don't matter nothin' what word you use? I know what we're doing. You know what we're doing."

"Yes, but it's all in the semantics, Stoney. Let's just say we're borrowing the cave balloons on a permanent basis." A pause, then, "At least they're going to someone who will value them."

"Borrowing on a permanent basis….I'll have to tell my probation officer that next time he tries to bust my chops." Stoney laughed harshly. "You can use all the fancy words you want, Ryan, but my probation guy would still call it stealing."

Stealing? Jack had just been about to yell out, but the word stopped him. "Wait a minute. Keep quiet," he murmured to Sam and Ashley, pressing his finger to his lips. "Shhhhh."

"So tell me about these balloon things you and I are 'borrowing permanently.' How come they're worth so much?"

The second person, who must be the "college boy," Jack figured, answered, "The real name for any cave specimens is 'speleothem.'"

"Speel—talk English," Stoney responded.

"Here's another word for you: hydromagnesite. That's what these little guys are made of. They are so rare—in the U.S., they're found in only eight caves, and in only three other caves in the whole world. Here in Carlsbad, there's only half a dozen of them in existence. That's what you call really rare."

Still whispering, Ashley said, "They must be scientists. They'll help us out. Let's—"

"No! Weren't you listening? They're a couple of thieves."

Ashley had begun to move forward when Jack grabbed her to stop her, just as the younger man was saying, "If my dad knew that I was lifting these cave balloons, he'd kill me."

"Yeah, but I figured you'd face death for some big bucks, Ryan," Stoney said. "Look at me—I'm willing to risk going back to the slammer for that kind of action. Five thousand greenbacks, split between you and me for a couple of cave specimens. That's what I call easy money."

"It's only easy if we don't get caught."

"Who's gonna tell on us—the stinkin' bats?" Another harsh laugh. "This is the same as robbing a cemetery—no one down in this big ol' grave can talk. It's perfect. And you're the perfect guy to do this."

Another pause, and then, "You know, I wanted to ask you, why me? How did you even think to call me?"

"Put two and two together. When I heard that collector talking about them balloon things at Tequila Joe's, I thought of you, 'cause I knew you work at that rock climbing place where all the cavers go. Word had gotten around that your dad'd fallen on hard times—"

"You heard about my dad losing his job?"

"People talk, Ryan. Especially in bars. So I figured you was just the type to need some extra cash. And—no surprise—I was right."

"But I've never done anything like this before," Ryan protested.

"There's always a first time, kid."

"The point is, I don't make enough in my summer job to pay for my car, let alone tuition. I need to go to school fall quarter. Sometimes the end has to justify the means, you know?"

"Whatever you say."

"I want you to know that this is the first, last, and only time—"

"Aw, quit blabbering. What's it matter if you steal a couple little rocks?"

"They're not just rocks. Collectors don't pay $5,000 for rocks! Take a look at them in the light."

Keeping a hand on Sam's shoulder to make sure he'd stay quiet, Jack tried to figure out what to do. If he went forward and interrupted two men in an act of theft, he could be in greater danger than just waiting in a cave until rescue came.

The younger one, Ryan, was saying, "A hydromagnesite surface is only about a tenth of a millimeter thick. Inside, these little balloons are filled with a kind of gas. If you didn't know they were hollow, you'd think they were pearls. That's what they look like, sort of—about the same size as large pearls."

"They're worth a lot more than pearls, my man."

"That's exactly why I have to be real careful cutting them loose. One bad move, and they could be crushed."

Ashley whispered. "What should we do? Wait here till they're done, and then follow them out?"

"Do nothing. Just keep quiet," Jack whispered back. "They're crooks. They could have guns."

The man with the deeper voice asked, "So how do you know about these caves and rocks and stuff?"

The answer drifted back, "I've been a caver since I was six. My dad started me out here, exploring Carlsbad, then all the other caves here in the Guadalupe Mountains. That's why my dad would kill me if he knew what….Hey, you know what? I'm feeling pretty bad about it, too."

"Don't go all soft on me."

Ryan answered, "I can't talk anymore. I gotta concentrate on what I'm doing."

So, Jack thought, they had stumbled onto criminals. First he'd gotten them lost, and now he'd brought Sam and Ashley face-to-face with a new and different danger. His breath caught as he realized the trouble they could be in.

Ashley grabbed Jack's arm and whispered, "This is great. Now we'll be able to get out of here. We can follow these guys out."

Jack considered this. It was true Ryan said he was familiar with Carlsbad and the Guadalupe Mountains. But would it be safe to try to trail after two cave robbers? The one with the deep voice had even been in prison!

"Come on, Jack, it's the only way. I think we ought to sneak up a little closer to them," Ashley went on softly.

"Why?"

"What if they start to leave and we don't know it—then we'd miss our chance to follow them. Jack, you know we can't stay here. Look at the candle."

When Jack saw there was hardly more than a quarter inch of wax left, he realized she was right. They needed to get close enough to the robbers to know when they were about to leave the cave, yet keep out of their sight in case they turned out to be dangerous.

"OK," he whispered. "But we gotta be really careful." Bending down so that his lips were next to Sam's ear, he asked, "Do you understand what's happening? Those are bad guys, but when they get ready to leave, we can follow them. As long as they don't see us."

Though Sammy nodded, Jack could feel him trembling.

"So we'll stay real, real quiet. I'll go first, then you, then Ashley."

The three of them crept forward. As soon as they reached the point where Jack noticed dim illumination farther ahead, he blew out the sputtering candle, both to save the little bit of it that was left and to keep the men from noticing it. Sam clutched his hand in a painful grip, digging his fingernails into Jack's palm. When Jack pulled his hand away, Sam clutched the back of Jack's sweatshirt instead.

Each step was a conscious decision, a careful lifting of the foot and an even more careful placing of it on the cave floor. Jack knew that Ashley was moving as cautiously as he was. But Sam, clinging to Jack's belt now, shuffled along behind him, terrified of the dark. Then, one of them—it must have been Sam—kicked a stone.

"What the crud was that?" the deep-voiced man demanded.

"Sounds like something fell," Ryan answered.

"Nothin's gonna fall in this cave by itself. Someone's gotta be back there."

"There's no one in this cave, Stoney. That's impossible. It's after hours. No one could get in unless they jimmied open the locked door like we did."

"Nothin's impossible. We need to check it out."

In the blackness, Jack, Sam, and Ashley froze, not even breathing.

They heard footsteps coming toward them. Suddenly two brilliant, luminous eyes, 12 inches apart on what looked like an enormous head, drilled into them from no more than 20 feet away.

"The Chupa—!" Sam screamed. "Ch-chupa—G-g-g-goat...."

"Sam—no!" Jack cried.

But Sam had bolted, running crazily away from them, his feet churning in the soft cave dirt until he disappeared into darkness.

A voice said, "It's kids. I saw them. Three kids."

"Where did they come from?"

"Over there—on your right!"

The two stabbing lights were not eyes, but two individual headlamps, one on each of the men. Since the men were about the same height, when they stood side by side, the lights looked enough like a pair of eyes to scare Sammy out of his wits, making him think the Chupacabra had come after him. In the confusion, Ashley screamed, "Catch him! Catch Sammy! We can't lose him again."

Moving fast, the man named Stoney reached them, yelling, "What did you kids see?" as he grabbed Ashley's sore arm.

"Ouch! That hurts! Let me go! We didn't see anything.

It doesn't matter. We have to get Sammy before he gets lost again."

It was then that they heard a wild wailing, not too far away in the tunnel, about as far as a terrified eight-year-old might be able to run in little more than a minute.

"Come on, Stoney, let her go!" Ryan said. "It sounds like one of them's in trouble."

"Hey, you and me will be in trouble if these brats saw anything, and they go blabbing about it. I'm not going after some dumb kid and spoil what we got goin' here."

"You don't know this cave, and I do. It's dangerous," Ryan said as he pushed past Jack and Ashley to follow the sound of Sam's shrieks. "I'm not letting any little kid die in here."

"Hey, get back here, you!"

But Ryan was already moving rapidly along the tunnel, with Jack and Ashley running after him.

CHAPTER NINE

Stoney stayed behind, yelling, "Don't blow this job, man! Think of the money!" But Ryan pushed ahead, following the light of his headlamp as he unfastened a flashlight from his belt. When he turned that on, brightness flooded the cave as though a small sun had risen, and the sudden brilliance burned Jack's eyes, nearly blinding him. Jack still hadn't gotten a good look at either of the men, but he could tell that Ryan was thinner and younger than Stoney, and he wore a thick leather belt that all kinds of tools dangled from, like a repairman's. Ryan moved swiftly. The tunnel seemed to be as familiar to him as his own backyard.

"H-h-help! J-Jack!" Sam wailed.

"Hold on, Sam—we're coming!" Jack called out to the boy. Now that there was light to mark the path ahead, neither Jack nor Ashley had trouble keeping up with Ryan. They hurried behind his retreating figure.

Ryan stopped suddenly and turned to Jack, and this time, Jack could make him out clearly. He had pale blue eyes, the kind that looked almost colorless, and long orange-red hair pulled back into a ponytail. His skin was marked by a constellation of blemishes that reached all the way to his helmet.

"Is that the kid's name—Sam?" Ryan demanded. Jack nodded, while Stoney's rough voice barked, "Get back here. This is not our problem!"

Ignoring Stoney, Ryan turned once again down the narrow tunnel, his light sweeping in front of him in a brilliant arc. They hadn't gone too far when Ryan dropped to his knees, muttering, "I was afraid of this!" He shone the flashlight beam straight down into a hole that was about a yard long and less than two feet wide. Jack rushed to see, with Ashley crowding behind him.

"Stay back!" Ryan warned them. "One kid down in that pit is bad enough. I don't need another one falling on top of him."

It was Sammy down there! The strong flashlight beam lit his blond hair like a halo—but so far beneath them that Jack's jaw clenched. Earlier, Sam had lost his lantern in a pit alongside the tunnel path. Now Sam himself had fallen into yet another hole in the ground.

"Sam, this is Ryan speaking. Listen to me—I need to know if you are hurt."

"Uh-huh."

"Can you move your arms or your legs?"

There was a pause, and then, "Th-there's a r-r-rock p-pressing into my m-middle. It's hurting me."

"OK, I don't want you to move anymore. I want you to stay right where you are. Just hold on." Ryan sprawled on his stomach and held the flashlight into the hole as far as he could reach. After a moment, he pulled himself up, rocked back onto his thick boots and rested his flashlight across his knees. "Oh, man," he said softly, "this is bad."

"How far down is he?" Jack asked.

Ryan looked at him sharply. "About eight feet, I'd judge. He's probably got some scrapes and bruises, but it sounds like he's OK otherwise. I've fallen a lot farther than that without getting hurt too much. But that's not the problem."

"J-J-Jack—g-g-get me out of h-h-here," Sam wailed. "Hurry!"

"I will," Jack assured him. "I promise. It'll just be a minute." Then, to Ryan, "Do you have a rope or something? We've got to pull him up."

"We'll need more than a rope. He's jammed fairly tight—I could see it when I looked down. That's good."

"How is that good?" Jack demanded.

"Because that pit goes down another 75 feet, and if he hadn't gotten wedged, he'd be at the bottom right now."

It took a moment for Ryan's words to register. Ashley's eyes grew wide as she cried, "Are you saying he could fall the rest of the way?"

"Keep your voice down," Ryan hissed. "I don't want the kid to panic. His one foot's on a ledge that isn't very wide, so if he moves too much....You two will have to go and get a rescue team and bring them here. There's no other way. You need a professional team to save him."

"Great plan, except how can we do that?" Ashley threw her hands into the air. "We don't even know where we are! We've been trying to find our way out of this place for hours and hours!"

"J-J-Jack!" Sam called desperately. "My sh-shoe just fell off! It fell r-really f-f-far. I heard it wh-when it hit b-b-bottom."

"It's all right, Sam. We're working on a plan to get you out right now."

Coming up behind them, a deep voice rumbled, "I'm not doing squat for some brat, and you're not either!" Stoney had reached them. He was a pig-shaped person with a coarse beard and small eyes set back in his fleshy face. To Ryan, he snarled, "Man, get back there and do the job we came to do."

"Are you insane, or just stupid?" Ryan asked, incredulous. He was on his feet now, only inches from where Stoney stood. Stoney's thick legs planted into the cave floor like stalagmites, and his raised fists were clenched next to his barrel chest.

Stoney answered, "If the kids die here, so much the bet-ter, because if they get out and tell the cops about me, they're gonna die anyway. I'll come after them and kill them myself."

A chill of fear stabbed Jack's gut. Stoney's words were

probably no more than empty threats intended to scare them, and yet this guy looked mean enough to follow through on anything he said. Jack fought the urge to grab Ashley and run, to get out of there, to save himself by hiding somewhere in the tunnel. But there was Sam to think of. No, they couldn't leave. He just hoped he didn't look as scared as he felt.

"Shut up, Stoney," Ryan said. Although he was of slighter build than Stoney, Ryan seemed supple and athletic. Stoney backed up a step as Ryan told him, "You're a jerk, you know that? You don't care about anything except money."

"That's right."

"Starting right now, the deal's off, you hear me? I'm not gonna get those cave balloons for you to sell to your buyer. I never felt right about it from the beginning." Stabbing a finger into Stoney's chest, he said, "And if you try to get them yourself, you'll smash them like so many soap bubbles, so don't even try, because you don't have a clue how to do it. I'm telling you again just so you know I mean it— the deal's off. Finished. Over."

"You stupid—" Stoney began. "You know what? I was gonna cut you in on my DDT runs from Mexico—you're such a good talker, I figured you could do a snow job on the border police. But I ain't usin' no mush-hearted wimp. So Ryan, you just cut yourself out of not one but two sweet deals, you—college boy!" Stoney spat out the last two words.

"Get out of here," Ryan ordered. "You know the way."

Still snarling, Stoney answered, "You wanna be a bleeding heart? Go ahead, be a stupid bleeding heart. But how you gonna keep these brats from squealing on us when we get up to the top? I might go back to jail, but you'll pay a price. You'll get kicked out of school. You really want that?"

Too quickly, Ashley said, "We didn't hear anything. We don't know anything. We'd never squeal."

Stoney looked down at her, menace on his face. Moving as fast as a striking snake, he grabbed Ashley's sore arm and twisted it behind her back. "You'd better keep it that way. You turn me in and—"

"Let her go!" Jack yelled when Ashley turned pale with pain.

"Let her go!" Ryan repeated, his voice steely. "I'm gonna take these kids up to the surface. I don't give a rip what you do."

"J-J-J-Jack!" Sam shrieked from below them. "It's d-d-dark!"

"It's OK, Sammy," Jack cried. "We're going to get help. Just hold on!" Screwing up his courage, speaking in a voice that he tried to keep calm, Jack told Stoney, "Get us to the top, and we won't say anything to the rangers about you. You can trust me on that. Just let Ashley go."

"You can trust him," Ashley repeated through clenched teeth, "because he's a Scout."

At that, Stoney burst out in a guttural laugh. "Oh,

Boy Scout. I think my man Ryan here—he was a Boy Scout, too. Look how he turned out."

Ryan stood silent.

"You just remember, kid, I can find anybody if I want to. Think about that when you go talking to the rangers." He released Ashley's arm, giving her such a shove that she fell right into Ryan. Then Stoney turned on his heel and disappeared into the darkness. "Five thousand smackers down the tube," he shouted, the words echoing off the cave ceiling. "That's the last time I work a deal with a college kid. You might be getting educated, but you ain't got no smarts."

Ashley shrank back from Ryan and stood next to Jack. You all right? Jack mouthed. His sister nodded in reply.

Suddenly, Ryan seemed uncertain. Jack noticed how the flashlight in his hand trembled, and how his face flushed in fist-size blotches. He must have been more afraid of Stoney than he let on.

"Look…about the cave balloons…," Ryan stammered, "I…." He shook his head as if to clear his own thoughts. "No, we don't have time for this. We've got to go for help."

"Right! Let's go!" Jack said eagerly, ready to agree to anything that would get them out of this nightmare.

But a voice wailed from the pit, "J-J-Jack—d-d-don't g-g-go!"

"Jack, we can't go off and leave him," Ashley told him. "Both of us can't."

Jack gave Ryan a quick glance. "Ryan, could you—" but

Ryan held up his hands. "Sorry, I'll get you out of here and up to the top, but that's all I can do. One of you will have to bring the rangers back to your friend. I can't afford to get busted. So which one of you is it going to be?"

"Me. I'll go with you," Ashley said coolly. "Jack, you stay with Sam. He likes you more, anyway. I'll bring the rangers back."

"Then it's settled," Ryan said. "Let's go."

"Wait a minute!" Jack cried. Was he just going to stand there and let his sister go off with Ryan, a total stranger? And Stoney was still somewhere in the cave, a convicted criminal mean enough to twist his sister's arm. What had he been in jail for? Theft? Assault? Murder? And how did Jack know that Ryan would really help them? After all, he'd come down here to steal cave specimens.

"Wait a minute for what?" Ryan asked him impatiently. "We don't really have a minute."

Jack felt like he was being torn to pieces by tigers. All his instincts pushed him toward going with Ashley, not only because he was afraid to let her leave with a stranger, but—he had to admit it—because he was so desperate to get out of that cavern himself. But what about Sam? Jack couldn't just walk away and leave Sam all alone in the bottom of a pit.

"Look," Ryan was saying, "that kid down there needs help fast because his muscles will get stiff from the cold and he won't be able to hold on. This girl—she's your sister, right?—has got to bring the rescue team here. Like I just said, I'm not going to stick around and get busted." As though trying to convince himself, he added, "I'm doing the right thing because I'm really a decent guy. I almost made a mistake, but now I'm turning back. But I gotta do it fast and walk away from it because I don't want this to go wrong and ruin the rest of my life. I'll help you as much as I can, but that's all I can do. Understand?"

Yes, Jack understood. Ryan would lead Ashley to the surface, then disappear while Ashley went for help.

"How's the rescue team gonna know where we are?" Jack asked. "We don't even know where we are, so how can Ashley tell them?"

"Easy. She'll tell them it's where the hydromagnesite balloons are located in Left Hand Tunnel. The park geologist will know exactly where that is."

"But it's late," Jack objected. "The park geologist might have gone home."

Losing patience, Ryan said, "Enough! Shut up! If you want that kid down there to be rescued, we need to get moving. Here, keep my headlamp so you won't be in the dark. Just stay here and keep talking to the kid. And keep him talking. It's important. And be sure to tell him not to move!"

And then they were gone—Ryan in the lead, Ashley right behind him, staying so close she nearly stepped on Ryan's heels. With more fear and foreboding than Jack had ever before felt in his life, he watched them disappear, the light from Ryan's flashlight growing dimmer and dimmer until they turned a corner and it was gone.

"J-J-Jack," Sammy called, sounding weaker now.

Keep him talking, Ryan had said. But how do you do that with a kid who can hardly talk in normal circumstances?

"I'm here, Sammy. I'm bringing a light. Ryan—he said to remind you not to move. Try to stay exactly where you are."

Jack went to where the pit loomed and dropped onto his stomach. Tipping the light so that it shone on top of Sam's head, he noticed rock formations jutting out like rows of blunted teeth. It was as if Sam had dropped into the jaws of a predator. Jack watched silt catch the light before it settled on Sammy's head. Was it Jack's imagination, or had Sammy slipped even farther down? He could feel his own fear twist inside him.

"See. I've got a light. It's not dark anymore," he said, trying to keep his voice even. "Ryan left it for us. It's a headlight attached to webbing that fastens around your head so you can see—you know?—without having to hold a light in your hands. I think it's even brighter than a regular flashlight. Anyway, Ashley's gone with Ryan, and she'll bring back help. You don't have to worry—I'm staying here with you."

"M-my stomach h-hurts."

"Mine, too. Must have been that granola bar we ate. It had to be at least a year old." Jack's joke sounded feeble, even to him. What if Sam were bleeding internally? What if he were about to slip into a coma? "Sam," he called, louder this time, "can you hear me?"

Silence.

"I need you to talk to me. I need to know you're OK."

"I-I'm s-s-sorry, J-J-Jack." Sam's voice sounded far away. "M-m-my f-fault."

"What? What's your fault?"

"Th-th-this."

"Nah, nobody's to blame. You just got scared. I run when I'm scared. I thought those headlamps were creepy, too. But they weren't eyes. They were not a Chupacabra. Just lights. I don't think there's any such thing as Chupacabras. They're just stories people make up, like fairy tales."

Sam didn't say any more, so Jack tried to fill in the empty space with his own prattling. It was as if his words were tiny fishhooks that he could throw down to Sam, hooks that could grab him and lift him from danger. "Accidents happen, Sam. Things go wrong. And sometimes it's not anybody's fault, you know? I've made lots of mistakes in my life, but mostly it all works out OK. It'll be the same for you." Jack listened for a reply, but heard none. "Hey, can you hear me?"

"Y-yes."

"Good. I don't want to have a conversation with myself. Help me out here."

"You d-d-don't make m-m-mistakes."

Jack gave a loud guffaw. "Sure I do. All the time."

"Wh-when?"

"It was a mistake to stop back there in the cave and just sit around, waiting. No one came for us—it probably would have been better to keep going. I don't know. And I get scared, sometimes over stupid things. You want to know something? When we first came here, I was afraid of the bats. That was really dumb because the bats haven't hurt me at all. In fact, if we could have followed them fast enough, they would have led us out of here. You were never afraid of the bats, were you?"

"N-no."

"Well, see there—from the start you were braver than I was. Except now I don't think I'm scared at all anymore. I think bats are pretty cool." Jack paused and reflected on this, since what he'd just said was true. He wasn't afraid anymore. When had that happened?

"M-my m-m-mom s-s-said...." Sam's voice choked off.

"What? What did she say?" Jack moved his face even farther over the edge, holding the lamp awkwardly so that he could get a better view of Sam. Sam squirmed, pushing back his head so that his eyes were barely visible, like two slivers of half moons, as he stared up at Jack. "S-she s-s-said...sh-she s-s-said....I'm a l-l-loser."

Jack felt bile rise in his throat. "Your mom told you that?"

"Sh-she al-al-always says it. All the t-t-time."

"Well," Jack snapped, "she's wrong."

He could tell Sam didn't believe him. Well, why should

he? He'd been told one thing for eight years, and it would take a lot more than Jack's positive thinking to undo the knots in Sam's life. Sam's experience was so completely different from his own. Jack's life was well-ordered, like his camera and lenses—everything made sense, everything locked into a pattern, everything fit. His parents needed him. His sister needed him. What would it be like to live in a world where the very people he looked at to define himself told him he was worthless? Once again, having a foster kid thrust into Jack's life brought everything else about his life into sharp focus.

"Sam, you're a Mini-Me, right? And I'm not a loser."

"She t-t-took d-d-drugs because of m-me."

"No, she took drugs because of her. Don't go getting yourself sucked in to stuff like that. That's a bunch of garbage. I wouldn't lie to you."

A strangled cry escaped from the rocks beneath him. "I-I c-c-can't even t-t-talk right. I c-c-can't d-do anything r-r-right. When I b-b-bring her m-matches, she th-throws them a-a-away. She h-h-hates me. You d-d-don't know m-me. I'm n-not l-like you. That's a j-j-joke. I g-g-got us l-lost. I c-c-can't—I h-hate—"

"Stop it! Stop talking like that. I mean it, Sam!" Jack held the lamp farther down so that the light flooded over Sam. His face was invisible now. Head bowed, his shoulders shaking with sobs, wedged in between rocks, Sam seemed so small. Even though Jack was right there, he could tell Sam felt alone.

Jack felt helpless. Totally helpless.

."J-Jack!" Sam cried. "H-help me! What if I fall?"

CHAPTER TEN

Jack heard them before he saw them—first the sound of people's voices, then the shuffle of footsteps and the clatter of equipment. And at last, the blessed sight of light, lots of light, coming from at least a dozen headlamps. The rescue team had arrived!

Pushing himself to his knees and then straightening his chilled body to an upright position, Jack felt surprise when he saw the rescuer in the lead. Wearing Park Service gear, this ranger had to be a grown man because he had a thick, full mustache, but he looked no bigger than a boy—in fact, not nearly as tall as Jack.

"Hi, I'm Boomer," the man announced, "and these guys are the rescue crew." Without wasting another word on Jack, Boomer peered down into the pit and called, "Hello down there. What's your name, fella?"

"His name's Sam," Jack answered.

In a quiet but no-nonsense voice, Boomer told Jack, "I know that, but I want him to tell me." And then, louder, "Hey, mister. My name's Boomer. What's yours?"

"S-Sam S-S-Sexton," the muffled reply came up.

"Pleased to meet you, Sam. You know what? I came here to bring you out of that hole." Boomer sounded so totally confident that no one could have doubted he'd do what he said.

He went on, "I'll be down there before you know it, Sammy." Then, to the people behind him, he murmured, "This won't be hard, if we can just get him to stay still. But if he moves, he could drop. Start setting up the rigging."

With practiced efficiency, looking as though they'd performed rescues like this dozens of times, the team began putting together ropes and clips, pulleys and snap links. A uniformed woman told Jack to move back in order to give the rescue team room to operate.

"Where's my sister and my parents?" Jack asked her.

"They're waiting in the lunchroom. You'll see them soon."

"Why didn't they come to find us? We've been lost for"—he looked at his watch—"almost eight hours now."

She answered, "Because several people from the tour group swore they saw you three kids ride up in the elevator with the group. Everyone's been searching for you aboveground. Those witnesses were so certain, so sure they saw you going into the visitor center, that no one suspected you were still in the tunnel." She shrugged. "Must have been three other kids. So much for the accuracy of eyewitnesses. But that's all the questions for now, Jack. Stay back, and let us do our job." As she spoke, three of the other rangers kept laying out a complex mass of rescue equipment—ropes, carabiners, pulleys, webbing, and other hardware.

Jack moved a little bit away, but he didn't want to get too far from Sam, who kept calling to him, although Sam's cries began to quiet as Boomer kept up a steady barrage of talk. "Bet you're cold, Sam, right?" Boomer was saying. "Well, I'm going to bring you a hat to wear. It won't be a hat with earmuffs, it'll be a hard hat like I have on, like all the rest of these people are wearing. Can you see us, Sammy? You'll get to wear a helmet just like ours, with a light on it. You'll like that, won't you?"

Sam's voice drifted up. "Uh-huh."

"I already told you what my name is, Sam. It's Boomer. Do you think that's a funny name? Bet you never met anybody with that name before." As he spoke, Boomer was putting on a harness of nylon webbing, stepping into the two leg loops and connecting it in the front with a carabiner. "Sam, I want to ask you a question. When you went into that hole, did you fall down or did you kind of slide down?"

"S-s-slide," Sam answered.

"You didn't just drop ka-boom, right? It was more like a real, real steep sliding board, and you went feet first? Or did you go headfirst?"

"F-f-feet."

"That's good. Very good."

"He's standing on a ledge," Jack said.

"I can see that," Boomer answered briefly. With everyone but Sammy, Boomer's words were sharp and to the point. With Sam, he kept up that stream of cheerful chatter. "Now Sammy, you're holding on to some rocks, and that's just what I want you to keep doing. Keep on holding them."

"OK."

Speaking again to the other members of the rescue team, Boomer said, "He's standing upright, holding tight to rock outcroppings, and he doesn't seem to have any broken bones. I'll need a fixed main line and a prusik minding belay." Those terms didn't mean anything to Jack, but that didn't matter because Boomer said next, "I'm going down to talk him up." And to Sam, in that much warmer voice, "Sam, I want you to do something for me. You have to pay attention to what I'm going to tell you. I'm coming down to get you, but I want you to just stay real still till I get there. Understand? Don't move at all. Keep holding on to those rocks. When I get close to you, don't reach up to me. Don't try to jump up to me. Do you hear what I'm saying?"

"Yes."

"That's a good boy. Will you promise me, Sam, that you won't reach up when I get close to you? You'll just keep holding on to those rocks?"

"P-promise."

In a low voice to the woman who'd moved Jack out of the way, Boomer said, "I'm checking the rescue rigging, ready to rappel." As he moved to the edge of the pit, he asked, "On belay?"

"Belay on," she answered.

"On rappel," Boomer said, and began his descent over the edge, telling Sam, "Here I come. Keep holding those rocks. You're doing so great! I'm real proud of you. Real, real proud."

Very quickly, Boomer disappeared into the hole. From where Jack was standing he couldn't see a thing, and when he tried to move forward, one of the rescue team shook his head and signaled for Jack to move back again. But he could hear everything as Boomer kept chatting up Sam: "Just look how you're holding on to those rocks, Sammy. That's really good. You could be a mountain climber. Or you could be a caver, which is even more fun."

As he dropped lower, he became just a bit harder to hear. "Now I'm right behind you, Sam." The words came up slightly muffled. "See this thing I'm snapping around you? It's a harness, sort of like the one I'm wearing. And I've got a piece of rope that will clip our two harnesses together. Know what the rope is called? It's called a cow's tail."

And then Jack heard a sound he'd never expected to hear. Sam was laughing! "C-c-cow's tail," he repeated.

"Yeah, as in moooo. How old are you, Sam? About 15?"

"Eight," Sam answered.

"No kidding! You're doing such a great job, I thought you were much older. Here's a hat for you to put on. Do you like it? It fits you pretty good, doesn't it? See, it's got a light on it just like mine. Now, we're going to go up. I want you to put your hands and feet exactly where I tell you to. See that rock right there? Grab it with your right hand."

"I'm a l-l-lefty," Sam told him.

"Hey! Really? I'm a leftie too. Lefties are usually very smart people, so two smart lefties like us won't have any trouble getting out of this hole. On belay?" he called up.

A crew member at the top responded, "Belay on."

"Grab that rock up there with your left hand," Boomer was telling Sam, "and your right foot goes… right…there!"

Jack watched a crew member keeping tension on the line to Sam's harness, but he really wished he could see Sam and Boomer ascending the rock wall. Hearing Boomer's words was the next best thing. "This rope will hold 6,000 pounds. You don't weigh more than that, do you, Sam?"

"No!" Another giggle from Sammy. Minutes later, he was being lifted into the waiting hands of the rescue team members, the yellow hard hat tilted a bit askew on his head.

"You made it, Sam!" everyone congratulated him. "What a brave boy! Now we're going to get you out of here." As they spoke, they were wrapping Sam in blankets.

The woman who'd kept Jack away from the edge seemed more relaxed now, so Jack asked her, "Can I go to him?"

"Not yet," she answered. "The EMTs—emergency

medical technicians—need to check him. If he slid down into that hole like he says he did, he's probably got a lot of scraped skin on the front of him. We'll get him up to First Aid right away. And you, too. You need to be checked at First Aid."

"I'm all right," Jack told her. "I just want to see my mom and dad."

Jack was amazed at how quickly they reached the lunchroom—it was all a matter of knowing which path to take, he realized. He and Sam and Ashley had been a lot closer to safety than they knew when they were lost in the blackness, running scared.

The wooden door swung open to reveal a whole crowd of people waiting anxiously in the brightly lighted lunchroom. "There they are!" Olivia cried, and almost in a single leap she caught Jack in her arms, asking, "Are you all right? We were frantic! Is Sam all right?"

"Looks like everyone's fine," Boomer answered. "Cold, no doubt, and hungry for sure, but nothing that a few Band-Aids and a bowl of hot soup won't fix, I bet. But I'm no doctor, so the kids need to be checked over."

Boomer didn't ride up in the elevator with them; it was the EMTs who took charge, counting the seconds as the elevator quickly rose 754 feet, then hustling them into the First Aid room right next to the elevator lobby. Once inside First Aid, Sam was examined thoroughly. "I d-didn't g-get to say good-bye to B-B-Boomer," he complained.

"I bet you'll see him again," Olivia assured the boy, and then went on to tell Jack how worried they'd been when they learned that Consuela had collapsed and the three of them had disappeared, a worry that escalated into panic and then desperate fear as the hours passed and they weren't found.

"Can you believe it!" Steven exclaimed, "At the end of the tour, not two but three different people—two women and a man—swore you three kids went up on the elevator with them. They must have mistaken you for other kids on the tour. Because of that, the searches were concentrated up here, aboveground—in the visitor center, the staff offices, the parking lot, the trails....No one thought to look in the cave because the witnesses—three of them!—had been so positive. With all the excitement over Consuela, it's easy to see how people could become confused."

"And then," Olivia broke in, "just at the time the search team decided they really ought to check Left Hand Tunnel, at that very moment, Ashley appeared." Her voice breaking, she reached for her daughter and murmured, "And Ashley told us where you were."

Jack wanted to ask about Ryan, but he thought he'd better not, not with all those law-enforcement rangers around. Instead, he asked, "What happened to Consuela? Was she really on—" He hesitated to use the word "drugs."

"Oh, you haven't heard about that part, have you," Steven answered. "We told Ashley, but I forgot that you didn't know about Consuela. She's a diabetic, Jack. From the way we reconstructed it, she took her insulin injection the way she was supposed to before lunch, but then she never got to eat her lunch because some tourists kept talking to her. That's what led to an insulin reaction."

"You mean—just because she didn't get enough to eat?" Jack could hardly believe that medicine that was supposed to help someone could cause that person to act the way Consuela had. "That's what made her talk funny? And then faint?"

Steven nodded. "It's what can happen to people with diabetes. Consuela had a bracelet that identified her as a diabetic—she wore it for emergencies. She felt awful when she got back to normal and realized that she'd left you kids without supervision. And when it turned out that no one knew where you were, she was devastated."

One of the EMTs came up to Olivia then and said, "The little boy seems fine, but we still want to drive him to the hospital in Carlsbad for x-rays, just to make sure he didn't sustain any internal injuries when he fell. He's got a good-size bruise on his stomach."

"Of course," Olivia answered. "Are you taking him in the ambulance? Shall I ride in the ambulance with him?"

"I want Jack," Sam declared, dangling his legs over the edge of the examination table. He still wore the hard hat. Reaching up, he kept switching the headlamp on and off. The insides of his bare arms showed a multitude of red scratches where the jagged edges of the rock formations had dug into him as he slid into the pit. Fortunately, the fake-leather jacket he'd worn had protected him from worse cuts. The jacket lay across a chair, its sleeves and front in shreds. On top of the jacket sat a single shoe. Jack wondered how long Sam's other shoe would stay in that dark pit. Forever?

It was like a reunion the next morning in Dr. Rhodes's office. "I really wish I had more chairs," she apologized. Consuela stood leaning against a wall, Boomer sat on the edge of Dr. Rhodes's desk, the three kids were cross-legged on the floor again, and as the only guests who'd been given chairs, Steven and Olivia looked a little sheepish.

"Sammy, I like your new shoes," Consuela told him.

"They're Air J-Jordans," Sam answered, brushing an invisible speck of dirt from the toe of one of them.

"Well," Dr. Rhodes said, "since you Landons will be leaving New Mexico tomorrow, there are lots of things we need to clear up before you go. First, just as a matter of interest, Consuela got a letter from her cousins in Mexico. Consuela, why don't you tell the Landons what your cousin wrote in that letter."

Almost shyly, Consuela answered, "I hate to use the words, because I don't want Sammy to be scared again...."

"He won't be. Sam's a brave boy," Boomer declared, reaching out to tap lightly on the top of the yellow hard hat, which Sam still wore. The rangers were allowing him to keep it.

"The letter was about…vampire bats," Consuela told them. "In Mexico. There aren't so many of them, but the farmers and ranchers hate them because even though their numbers are small and the bats themselves aren't very large, they feed on the blood of cattle and sometimes cause rabies. So the ranchers in my cousins' area have been searching out all the caves where the bats roost. Then they drag old tires into the caves and set them on fire."

Dr. Rhodes took over, "The toxic smoke from the burning rubber chokes the bats, and they die. The problem is, our Mexican free-tailed bats from here at Carlsbad fly across the border into Mexico and often roost there in the same caves as the vampire bats. So they're being killed, too, by toxic vapors from the burning tires."

"And you think that adds to the decline of the bat population here at Carlsbad?" Olivia asked.

"It's one of the reasons. Of course, a bigger reason is the pesticides. Especially DDT. As you know, the bats fly back and forth across the border to Mexico. In the United States, DDT is illegal, but Mexico still uses it to control mosquitoes that spread malaria. Here in this country ranchers can't buy DDT even if they want to."

Jack sat up straight. "Wait a minute," he said. "Last night we heard that man, Stoney, talk about bringing DDT into the U.S. from Mexico. Does that mean he's smuggling it in so ranchers can get it here?"

"You heard him say that?" Boomer asked. "You heard this guy Stoney admit he's sneaking DDT across the border? Wow! This is important. We need to find him."

Quietly, Ashley said, "If you want to find him, just ask Ryan. He'd probably tell you where Stoney is, because he feels so bad that Stoney almost pushed him into stealing the cave balloons. Ryan's really sorry about that, he told me."

"Seems you learned a lot about Ryan, Ashley," Boomer commented.

Ashley murmured, "He...talked. He tried to explain."

Looking intently at Ashley, Boomer asked slowly, "Do you know how we could contact Ryan? I mean, I saw him for a minute when he brought you to us, but he disappeared pretty fast."

Ashley dug a small piece of paper out of the pocket of her jeans, but kept it in her hand while she murmured, "He gave me his telephone number. He made me promise I'd call him after the rescue to let him know that Sam was all right, because he was scared that Sam might fall into the pit. And I did. After we went back to the motel in Carlsbad last night, I called Ryan. I just didn't tell anybody."

In the silence that followed, no one reached to take the piece of paper. Then Dr. Rhodes leaned forward to ask gently, "Do you feel you'd be betraying your rescuer if you let us contact Ryan, Ashley? It may save a lot of lives—lives of bats, I mean. If ranchers in this area are using DDT that Stoney's bringing across the border, that could be why some of our bats are vanishing."

Hesitant, Ashley held out the paper, but only partway. "As long as Ryan won't get into trouble," she answered. "After all, he saved our lives."

"I think I can guarantee he won't be arrested and charged with anything," Boomer assured her. "Ryan didn't commit any major offense last night. He just went into the cavern after hours, which would be considered trespassing. We would overlook that if he'd help us nail Stoney, because Stoney might lead us to other DDT smugglers."

With her eyes cast down, Ashley thought it over. Then, almost reluctantly, she gave the paper to Boomer.

Suddenly, loudly, Sammy declared, "Ryan didn't s-save my life. It was B-Boomer who saved my l-l-life!"

That broke the tension, and everyone relaxed. "You're right, Sammy. That added one more rescue to Boomer's long list of amazing heroics," Dr. Rhodes told them. "You should hear what else this man has done!" As she went on to describe Boomer's exploits, the Landons' eyes grew wide and their jaws dropped in astonishment.

Boomer, it turned out, was so small because in the seventh grade, he'd been stricken with a kind of rheumatoid arthritis that eventually fused his spine and took all the cartilage from his shoulders. He'd had two hip replacement operations and a heart valve repaired. Yet Boomer had earned an airplane pilot's license, he taught rappelling to cavers and climbers, he'd performed dozens of heroic rescues that were far more dangerous than his rescue of Sam, and not only that, he was famous for discovering and exploring new caves in Carlsbad Cavern.

"Tell them about the cave they named after you," Consuela urged him. "Bemis Chamber."

Grinning modestly, Boomer said, "I got to explore that cave because I was the only one small enough to fit. There was this really tight passage about eight feet long, and it went straight down. I had to inch through it, with one arm stretched forward and the other arm tight against my side, to minimize my diameter. It wasn't so bad getting into the cave, because the passage was downhill, so it took me only about 20 minutes to go the eight feet. Getting back out, it was uphill, and that took me 45 minutes. Inch and wedge. Squeeze forward an inch, wedge yourself and try to breathe. It can feel kind of claustrophobic."

Grimacing at the memory, he continued, "I had to take off my shirt and belt to fit back up the hole. I was working so hard that the people outside the hole could hear my heart beat. When I got out, I could hardly stand up, I was so wet and cold."

"Ooooh!" Ashley looked at Boomer in wonder. Sounding a little breathless herself, she asked, "What was it like when you saw the cave for the first time?"

"Pure beauty!" Boomer exclaimed. "The chamber is about 35 feet long, 5 or 6 feet wide, and 20 feet high. The place where my feet first touched it was the only dry spot; everything else stood three feet deep in water. It's a 'living' cave. That means the formations are still growing. They look all wet and glossy, like marble carvings in a fountain. Whenever you see a cave with water dripping, that means it's still growing, and it's called a living cave."

"And they named that one after you?" Jack could only stare at this man who'd accomplished so much by sheer courage. What a guy! Then he glanced at Sam.

Sam seemed awestruck. He sat looking up at Boomer with intense admiration, but even more, with hope in his eyes.

Right away, Jack knew that he'd been replaced as Sam's idol. Sam had found a new hero in Boomer, and that was a good thing. Jack couldn't think of a more outstanding hero than this small man called Boomer, who possessed the heart of a giant.

CHAPTER ELEVEN

"It's like a m-m-magic world down h-h-here," Sam told them.

"So it is," Consuela answered, ruffing his hair until it stood up in soft tufts. "I'm glad I can see it with you."

"You ate your lunch th-this time?" Sam asked. "You're not s-s-ick?"

Consuela smiled and shook her head. "I finished my lunch, and I'm fine today. I'm really sorry I frightened you, Sammy, and caused all that trouble. The thing is, I'm what's called a brittle diabetic. That means these insulin reactions can hit me really fast, without warning—I'm never even aware that they're happening. But from now on I'll be much more careful."

Sam nodded hard. "G-Good."

The Landons, Boomer, and Consuela were touring the Big Room in Carlsbad Cavern, a mile-and-a-half pathway that wound them through the most spectacular scenery Jack had ever experienced in his life. The Giant Chandelier, a huge formation made of ribbon stalactites, hung from the ceiling like sugar frosting. Popcorn-covered stalagmites, soda straws, and huge columns filled the vast space, which, according to Boomer, was the largest natural limestone chamber in the United States. "The Big Room is shaped like a cross, with the long part being around 1,800 feet and the T part 1,100 feet at the widest point. It covers 8.2 acres, with the ceiling 255 feet high at its greatest point," he'd told them as he led them onto the winding pathway. "It's a natural wonder."

"It's so beautiful," Ashley breathed as they looked out over glittering gypsum. "I feel like we're walking into a giant wedding cake. That's what they should call it: 'Place of the Wedding Cake'."

"Nah, that sounds way too girly. How about we call it 'Goblins of the Underworld'," Jack countered.

Ashley wrinkled her nose. "No way," she told him. "The Bride's Chamber."

Unfolding a brochure as they walked, Jack pointed and said, "Look, the map says up ahead we'll be in the Hall of Giants. That's a good name."

"But I see ice-cream cones and crystals and cave roses and all kinds of pretty things," Ashley murmured whimsically.

"And I see gargoyles and orcs and gremlins," Jack shot back.

"I'd say you're both right," Boomer told them. "Up ahead is a place called Fairyland. And there's another spot called Doll's Theater."

"See!" Ashley said triumphantly. "Nice names."

"But then there's other formations in here called the Witch's Finger and the Devil's Easy Chair. So there's something for everyone. Bet you'd like to see the Witch's Finger, wouldn't you, Sam?" Boomer asked him.

"You b-bet!" Sam answered happily. "I w-want to s-s-see everything!"

Sam shadowed Boomer, his face upturned toward Boomer like a flower to the sun. To their right walked Consuela. Olivia and Steven, dressed in gray sweatshirts emblazoned with the name Carlsbad Caverns, followed behind, while Ashley and Jack tagged along in the rear.

"You want to see a witch's finger?" Steven asked Sam. "Boy, it doesn't seem like you get scared of anything anymore!"

"Nope. Boomer's not s-scared, and I'm l-like him."

"Now, I didn't say I never get scared," Boomer corrected. He stopped and leaned against the metal railing, his hands dangling over the side. "There's plenty in these caves to frighten a person. You have to respect a place like this. Sometimes being afraid means you're just plain old smart."

Nodding again, Sam said, "Boomer and m-me, we're b-both smart. That's 'cause we're l-l-lefties. Did you know, Jack, that lefties are s-smarter than other p-p-people?"

"No, I didn't know that," Jack answered. He seriously doubted there were any hard facts to support that theory, but he might as well let Sam believe it if he wanted to. Sometimes it was tactful just to keep quiet.

Other times it was more difficult to decide when to speak up. After a lot of wrestling with her own conscience, Ashley had handed over Ryan's telephone number. Later she'd whispered to Jack that if Ryan got into trouble she'd feel terrible, but she was trying to save some bats' lives.

"Ryan will be fine," Jack had assured her. And he believed that.

Maybe Ashley was connecting to his thoughts again, as she did so often, because she said, "If I were a bat, I'd love to live in this incredibly beautiful Big Room. But you know, when I think of Carlsbad, I'll always remember Left Hand Tunnel. When we were lost in the dark there, I didn't get too panicked, but the one thing that really freaked me out was those lights on the bats. They looked like glowing eyes, and for a minute I thought they were flying goblins or something."

Consuela explained, "Those lights you saw were little tags that had been glued to the fur between the bats' shoulder blades." Dressed in blue jeans and a crisp, white shirt, Consuela looked healthy and strong, and her words sounded perfectly clear. "The bats you found in the right fork of Left Hand Tunnel are not Mexican free-tailed bats," she continued. "We knew we had small colonies of fringed myotis and cave myotis, but we didn't know exactly where in the cave they lived."

"People glue light tags on the bats?" Ashley asked incredulously. "Why?"

"It's an experiment to discover which route the bats are taking when they fly out of the caverns at night," Consuela answered. "The naturalists capture them in the cave, stick the light tags on, and then wait outside the different cave entrances to track the path of the bats."

"But won't those tag things hurt the bats?"

Olivia answered that one. "No, sweetheart, the light tags are just fluorescent markers like the light sticks you kids get at parties sometimes. Glow-in-the-dark stuff. They're real small, and they fall off after a couple of days."

Boomer added, "Light tags also let the naturalists see where the bats go to drink. We had no idea any of those rare bats were living in the right fork of Left Hand Tunnel—we just knew about the ones in the main part of the tunnel. When you kids told us that, you helped solve a bat riddle—and feed a Hodag at the same time."

"Hodag?" Jack asked.

"Hodag?" Ashley echoed.

"What's a Ho-d-dag?" Sam wanted to know.

Dropping his voice mysteriously, Boomer told them, "Hodags live in these caves. Now, I want you all to look up at the Spirit World." He pointed to a place high in the ceiling, so far away Jack could almost believe it stretched into another dimension. "We've got a family of Hodags living up there, but they won't hurt you. Much. Especially if you're real careful."

Sam frowned, but Jack could see the merriment in Boomer's eyes. "Oh yes, they're up there. In fact, they're all around us, hiding in the shadows. This cavern is the home of the original Hodag. Down at Lake of the Clouds, sitting out on a little peninsula, a Hodag waited for thousands of years, wondering is this all there is to existence? Then finally, man came. An Indian looked down into the entrance and saw the deep, dark cave. Then he slipped. As he screamed and fell into the entrance of the cave, adrenaline shot into his bloodstream, and the scent of the adrenaline came wafting down the slope, eventually reaching the nose of the Hodag. The Hodag sniffed"—Boomer made a large, snuffling sound, wiggling his nose—"and then he said, 'Something's changed, what is that smell? I think I'll call it...food.'"

"Ohhh, B-B-Boomer. That's just a st-story," Sam said, laughing.

"Since then, a Hodag's sole source of food is adrenaline," Boomer went on. "Hodags will do their best to scare the daylights out of cavers and get them to pump out that adrenaline into their bloodstreams. Hodags feed on people's fear."

"If they're r-real, then wh-what do they look like?"

"Well, it just so happens we've done a lot of research, so I can answer that question. The male Hodag has a red eyeball right in the middle of his forehead, and the female has a green eyeball. The Hodag colonies live way high up in the ceiling, and they stay warm by gathering the cloak of darkness around them. See those up there?" Boomer waved a thin hand toward the Spirit World. "Hodags are the dark spots in the ceiling."

Sam grinned. "Then why d-d-don't you go and catch one?"

"Can't. Hodags are an endangered species."

"Yeah. R-r-right."

"But I'm telling you, they're out there. All cavers know it." Boomer lowered his voice to a hoarse whisper. "If you're going through a chimney passage and get halfway up and that one solitary drop of water comes down and goes *pfft* and puts out the candle in your lantern, a Hodag did it. If you're going through a cave and no one else is around you and a rock comes rattling down from above, it's the Hodag that shoved the rock down. Oh yes, cavers have a healthy respect for Hodags."

"I still want to be a c-c-caver. 'Cause the Hodags— they're just m-m-make-believe. Like Goatsuckers."

"Good for you, Sam," Consuela told him. "You're absolutely right."

Boomer smiled so deeply that his cheeks looked as though they had pleats. "Sam, you're a very cool kid. You figured out that it was make-believe. And you know, if you don't let made-up stories like that scare you, then you'll learn to be brave all the time, even when bad things that are real happen to you."

The three of them—Sam, Boomer, and Consuela—drifted to another luminous formation. Olivia lingered behind, turning so that the small of her back rested against the railing, her hands clutching the cool metal. Steven draped his arm around Olivia's shoulders. Jack and Ashley huddled close.

"Does Boomer know about Sam's life?" Ashley asked. "He's so nice to Sam, it's kind of like he knows."

"Some," Steven told her. "He understands that Sam's had a pretty rough time of it. Boomer told me he's going to keep in touch with Sam. He said he'll teach him to explore caves next summer. Sam will be old enough then. Boomer told me he taught his oldest daughter to climb with ropes when she was only five."

After a moment, Olivia mentioned, "You two kids should know that Sam's not going back to live with his mother."

"He's not?" Jack exclaimed.

"Not right away. When we return to Jackson Hole, Sam's going to be placed in a long-term foster home while his mother's in rehab. If she can recover, she'll be required to take some parenting classes, and only after that will she get Sam back." Jack's face must have shown his feelings, because Olivia added quickly, "Ms. Lopez will make sure Sam is properly looked after. She's even lined up a speech therapist for him. Sam's going to be OK."

Well, Jack thought, all in all, it had turned out to be a pretty good trip. The problem of the bat decline might soon be worked out, the cave balloons were safe for now, and Sam had begun to believe he was a winner, not a loser.

"I know what we should call this cavern," Ashley declared softly. "We'll call it The Room of Dreams Coming True."

Jack nodded. Ashley had gotten it right this time.

n 1898, a 16-year-old named Jim White, who was just a couple of years older than Jack Landon, began exploring Carlsbad's hidden limestone caves. What drew him to the spot where he would make this amazing discovery? Bats! They caught the young Jim's attention as he was mending a fence—millions of Mexican free-tailed bats, swirling into the air like a black funnel cloud. It was that explosion of bats that led him across the desert landscape to the natural cave entrance, which Jim described as "the great hole under long slabs of yellow and gray stone." After making a ladder of sticks, rope, and wire, Jim entered the cave with only a lantern for light. What he saw, and what he later introduced to others, has become one of the true wonders of the world.

For 17 years after Jim's discovery, Carlsbad Cavern went mostly unnoticed. Although Jim was fascinated by his "Bat Cave," as he called it, records show that he wasn't much of a talker, and he had a hard time convincing others of the amazing underground world he had discovered. It didn't help that it was difficult to experience the cavern. Visitors had to be lowered 170 feet in buckets onto trails that were treacherous to walk, and it could take more than an hour to lower 20 people. Dedicated to luring visitors into the cave, Jim decided the Bat Cave needed better trails, so he began to level pathways and to string wire for handholds. Then, in 1915, Jim guided a Kansas-born photographer named Ray V. Davis into the cavern. Davis's amazing photographs of dazzling cave scenes began to arouse public interest, and visitors began appearing almost daily.

By 1923, the U.S. General Land Office sent an expedition to survey the cave's measurements. The leader of this expedition, Robert Holley, expected to be done with his assignment in a day. It took more than a month to finish the job. Holley, awed by glistening soda straws, delicate lily pads, mind-boggling spaces, and chandeliers made of ribbon stalactites, strongly recommended that Carlsbad Caverns be established as a national monument.

Several months later, a geologist named Dr. Willis T. Lee wrote an article for NATIONAL GEOGRAPHIC magazine, enchanting readers with descriptions of Carlsbad's natural wonders. On October 25, 1923, President Calvin Coolidge placed the caverns in the National Park System.

Since 1924, the first full year of operation, more than 37 million people have visited Carlsbad Caverns. And most of them, like Sam and Jack and Ashley and the rest of the

Landon family, have made the decision to help protect the caves and their formations, the bats and other animals, the plants and landscape, and the historical artifacts that have made Carlsbad Caverns a world heritage site. Many people come to Carlsbad Caverns to refresh their spirits, to learn more about nature and history, to broaden their horizons, or to share with their own children what their parents shared with them. Visitors like the Landons make it possible for us to preserve areas like Carlsbad Caverns for generations to come.

The portal to the vast wonderland of Carlsbad Caverns was known to prehistoric Native Americans 10,000 to 12,000 years ago. Although there is no evidence of any humans probing the depths of the cavern until Jim White's turn-of-the-century exploration, the early natives did leave behind a pictograph of a hand high up on the cavern's Natural Entrance wall, a lasting reminder of their spiritual connection to this mystical place.

May you one day explore the mystery and magic of Carlsbad Caverns for yourself.

Bob Hoff
Park Historian
Carlsbad Caverns National Park

ABOUT THE AUTHORS

An award-winning mystery writer and an award-winning science writer—who are also mother and daughter—are working together on Mysteries in Our National Parks!

ALANE (LANIE) FERGUSON'S first mystery, *Show Me the Evidence,* won the Edgar Award, given by the Mystery Writers of America.

GLORIA SKURZYNSKI'S *Almost the Real Thing* won the American Institute of Physics Science Writing Award.

Lanie lives in Elizabeth, Colorado. Gloria lives in Boise, Idaho. To work together on a novel, they connect by phone, fax, and e-mail and "often forget which one of us wrote a particular line."

Gloria's e-mail: gloriabooks@qwest.net
Her Web site: www.gloriabooks.com
Lanie's e-mail: aferguson@alaneferguson.com
Her Web site: www.alaneferguson.com

One of the world's largest nonprofit scientific and educational organizations,
the National Geographic Society was founded in 1888
"for the increase and diffusion of geographic knowledge."
Fulfilling this mission, the Society educates and inspires millions every
day through its magazines, books, television programs, videos, maps
and atlases, research grants, the National Geographic Bee,
teacher workshops, and innovative classroom materials.
The Society is supported through membership dues, charitable gifts,
and income from the sale of its educational products.
This support is vital to National Geographic's mission to increase
global understanding and promote conservation of our planet
through exploration, research, and education. For more information,
please call 1-800-NGS LINE (647-5463) or write to the following address:

NATIONAL GEOGRAPHIC SOCIETY

1145 17th Street N.W.
Washington, D.C. 20036-4688
U.S.A.

Visit the Society's Web site: www.nationalgeographic.com